MURDER
UNDER THE
MISTLETOE

MURDER UNDER THE MISTLETOE

A Canon Clement Mystery

The Reverend
RICHARD COLES

WEIDENFELD & NICOLSON

First published in Great Britain in 2024 by Weidenfeld & Nicolson
an imprint of The Orion Publishing Group Ltd
Carmelite House, 50 Victoria Embankment
London EC4Y 0DZ
An Hachette UK Company

1 3 5 7 9 10 8 6 4 2

A CIP catalogue record for this book is
available from the British Library.

ISBN (Hardback) 9781399621472
ISBN (eBook) 9781399621496
ISBN (Audio) 9781399621502

Typeset by Input Data Services Ltd, Bridgwater, Somerset

Printed in Great Britain by Clays Ltd, Elcograf, S.p.A.

www.weidenfeldandnicolson.co.uk
www.orionbooks.co.uk

IM

Elizabeth Coles

(who never surrendered the recipe)

Sitting under the mistletoe
(Pale-green, fairy mistletoe),
One last candle burning low,
All the sleepy dancers gone,
Just one candle burning on,
Shadows lurking everywhere:
Some one came, and kissed me there.

— Walter de la Mare

Chapter One

It was a crisp, cold morning that Christmas Eve, and the remains of a light dusting of snow lay over Champton St Mary, like icing sugar on gingerbread. The parish church was gloomy, save a faint light that flickered at the east end, and it was locked, for what was happening in that flickering light was not something that could be made public, or not yet.

A couple were kneeling together at the altar rail. How many couples had knelt where they knelt in the seven centuries or more of hatching, matching and dispatching, generation after generation after generation? This couple, however, were perhaps the unlikeliest.

Canon Daniel Clement, tall and greying, usually so calm, was anxious. Next to him was Detective Sergeant Neil Vanloo, fifteen years younger, looking like he had just come from rugby training.

Then Daniel said, 'I can't do this.'

'Yes, you can.'

'I *can't.*'

Neil grimaced. 'You can. We've been through this.'

'But I can't.' Daniel stood up. 'Every year the same. The tree goes up and the decorations come down. Every year I dress it with – if I may say so – impeccable taste. Every year I festoon it with little white lights. All I want is little white lights, shining steadily, like stars in the night sky. And every year I can't stop them from twinkling like Santa's grotto.'

They were each holding a little plastic box with a switch and two green, twisted cables that led to the tree, or rather to the two strings of Christmas lights that Daniel had carefully wound round it.

Among the relentlessly twinkling lights hung plain silver baubles 'donated' by the Motcombe Hotel, or rather by the Honourable Honoria de Floures, who was a wedding planner there when it suited her, and quite often resident at Champton House, half a mile from the rectory and her family's seat since the Norman Conquest.

'We need to apply method,' said Neil. 'First, let's find the "off" position.'

Daniel knelt again and they pressed and pressed the switches on their respective boxes until the lights were extinguished altogether.

'Good,' he said, 'now . . .' But as he spoke one strand began slowly to light up. He pressed the switch again, and Daniel pressed his switch again, and another erupted into fast blinks. They pressed and pressed again and soon the tree looked like it was infested with furious fireflies.

'Oh, blast,' said Daniel, 'and it's Christmas Eve . . .'

'Leave it with me, Dan. It's a blue job, not a pink job.'

Daniel, irritated, switched off the plug board and the tree was suddenly extinguished. 'What are blue jobs and pink jobs?'

'Blue jobs: fixing, electrics, self-assembly furniture. Pink jobs: mince pies, sermons, choir practice. Your sort of jobs. Can't you go and fetch out the three kings or something?'

'I suppose so. I really don't like to, though; they're not meant to arrive at Bethlehem until Epiphany.'

'When's that?'

'Sixth of January.'

'Bit late.'

'Not according to the ancient tradition of the Church. Christmas begins at midnight tonight and lasts until Epiphany, twelve days later.'

'Tell that to Braunstonbury Woolworths. They had the reindeer out on Remembrance Sunday.'

'I did a funeral last week and they'd put Christmas decorations up on the crematorium gates. I was sitting in the hearse with a grieving family in the car behind and when we drove through the gates Santa's sleigh lit up and played "Jingle Bells".' Daniel got up, a bit creakily, and flexed his knees. 'If you sort out the tree, I'll get Caspar, Balthazar and Melchior and then maybe you could help me do the stable?'

'Blue job,' said Neil, switching on the Christmas tree lights' unpredictable flicker again.

Daniel went to the flower room, inviolable domain of the Flower Guild, where his predecessor had expended a considerable amount of goodwill wresting some space on top of a cupboard from its baleful suprema, Stella Harper. Eventually she had agreed to accommodate the three kings for the 353 days of the year when their attendance was not required, but under protest: 'Where am I supposed to keep the oasis and chicken wire?' she had complained. 'In your vestry, Rector? No, I thought not. And it's really not suitable for the Kings ... they're plaster, aren't they? It's a wet environment, a *working* environment ...'

There had been another kingly contretemps in his own day, after Bob Achurch, the verger-cum-sexton-cum-tower captain, went on a course intended to stimulate children's ministry and came back unusually inspired. He decided to delight the youngest members of the congregation, and build anticipation for Christmas, by bringing out the three kings and – former Royal Marine that he was – deploying them in a strategic approach towards the crib, altering their position for each Sunday in Advent.

Daniel, caught between the rock of his punctiliousness and the hard place of wanting to look like he was empowering lay ministry, endured a fortnight before Anne Dollinger, Deputy Chairman of the Flower Guild, fortuitously fell over Balthazar and got rather nastily pricked by the basket of holly she was carrying. A health-and-safety assessment stalled the kingly progress and they went back to the top of the cupboard until Epiphany

He unfolded the mini stepladder, marked 'PROPERTY OF ST MARY CHAMPTON FLOWER GUILD' with DYMO tape, and brought the figures down. He unwrapped them on the counter: Caspar with his long white beard and gift of gold for a king; Melchior's beard grey, annoyingly chipped, with frankincense to mark the divine presence; Balthazar with myrrh for the tomb the baby would one day lie in. Balthazar, in this set, was black, following an ancient tradition, only the artist had made him look more like Al Jolson than a prince of Yemen; worse, he was presented in a crouch of obeisance, which Daniel's brother, Theo, last Christmas said would have pleased the KKK.

Time to retire him, Daniel thought; time to get someone to donate a new trio they could arrange around the crib without inviting that sort of criticism. He knew better than to put this to the Parish Church Council, which would immediately be roused by the criticism, defending the traditional set for no other reason than it was the traditional set and change was always bad. No, better if an unhappy accident befell him.

'Daniel?' Neil appeared in the doorway. 'I've done it.'

In the sanctuary, the tree's illuminations shone with an unblinking white light.

'Whatever you do, don't touch them,' said Neil. 'It's harder to sync than the Last Night of the Proms.'

'I'll leave them on,' said Daniel, taking out the little block of Post-it notes and the felt tip he kept in one of the capacious pockets in his cassock. 'DO NOT TOUCH' he wrote in capitals and stuck it on the control box. 'Shall we do the stable?'

Bob Achurch had fetched the stable from the shed outside in which it was stored along with the lawnmower, the maypole and the May Queen's garlands, which had rather withered in their forty years of fluttering. For convenience, the stable broke down into pieces, which could be stored flat, but putting it together was as complicated as assembling Chippendale's Diana and Minerva commode, and the method known only to Bob, who guarded such knowledge zealously.

The stable stood to the north of the chancel arch, uninhabited, with some straw strewn on the floor and an empty manger in the middle. A row of lights concealed by the gabled roof shed light on the Nativity scene that would soon occupy the space.

Together, Daniel and Neil collected the remaining cast of characters awaiting installation: Mary and Joseph, the shepherds, the ox and the ass, and some woolly sheep – not original to the set but which had been added to it by a long-departed Sunday School teacher in the Sixties, who had also introduced a gonk and a stuffed owl for a time until they were retired.

Together they placed them in a circle round the manger, adjusting them to get the sight lines right after Daniel noticed that Melchior was adoring the ox rather than the Christ Child – or rather, the space where the Christ Child should be.

'Where's the baby Jesus?' said Neil.

'The bambino doesn't appear until Midnight Mass.'

'Bambino?'

'The infant Jesus – in Italian. It's a High Church affectation I haven't quite been able to shake off yet.'

'Just one bambiiiinooo . . .'

'He's here.' Daniel took out a bundle of bubble wrap and newspaper containing the plaster figure of the infant Jesus, surprisingly white and blond for a native of the Middle East – another anomaly that should be corrected. 'We need to put him some-where safe until his big entrance.'

He was looking around for a suitable spot when suddenly the door from the vestry burst open. Two red-brown creatures, as sleek as otters, came barrelling into the chancel and ran in circles round Daniel's feet, squeaking with excitement, their tails wagging.

'Cosmo! Hilda! How did you get in?'

He had left the rectory dachshunds in the kitchen, whining at the back door when he left for church, put out that they would not be accompanying him to Matins. 'Stay!' he had said. 'It's Christmas Eve,' as if that were sufficient explanation. 'Be a good boy and a good girl!' he'd cooed, in the baby language he used for no other creature in all creation.

Their entrance was followed by his mother's, Audrey, wearing an apron so floury it gave what looked like a little puff of smoke when she patted it down. 'Daniel!' she said. 'Emergency!'

Half a mile away at Champton House, at the centre of the parkland that separated it from the rest of the village, Lord de Floures and the Honourable Honoria de Floures, the favourite of his three children, were sitting at either end of the splendid dining table in the Rudnam Room, named after the de Floures estate in Norfolk and hung with paintings of a former Lord de Floures' prized shorthorns. The table, which could seat fifty at its fullest five-pedestal extent, was currently configured to its shortest length, lest their guests at breakfast should feel isolated at its middle. On Bernard's right was a pale woman with immaculately set hair the colour of artisanal honey, dressed – or rather overdressed – in a Bill Blass pink pinstriped suit and rather more jewellery than was suitable for breakfast. She was trying to smother a grimace. Opposite her was a man once handsome, you could see, although the weight he now carried blurred his former sharpness and symmetry. He was wearing a three-piece suit in tweed that looked like the sort of thing an American might think was standard uniform for a winter visit to an English country house. The look was undone, however, by a pair of penny loafers that stuck out from his turn-ups as incongruously as clown shoes on a coroner. His hair – glossily black – also seemed wrong, too resistant to the years that had aged the rest of him.

The lady was Bernard's cousin Jane, who had grown up at Rudnam, left it as soon as possible, married into a fast set in London, then remarried into a faster set in New York and now lived with the man sitting opposite her, her third husband, Victor Cabot, on the Upper West Side, 'between Columbus and Amsterdam', which made Bernard think of galleons rather than brownstones. Her Christmas at Champton was quinquennial, or thereabouts, to spend time with her English cousins and refresh her sense of the grandeur and antiquity of her heritage. It was also intended to remind her husband of his great good fortune when she consented to be his wife – a pearl beyond price, or very nearly beyond price. Jane had never been a low-maintenance kind of girl.

She was grimacing because Bernard, or Bunny

as she alone called him, had invited them to join the family in their pew at church on Christmas morning.

'*Such* a celebration,' she said, 'and so *exhaustive*.' Last night they had endured the annual Champton House carol concert. A choir with a small but noisy brass ensemble had been crammed onto the great staircase, its banisters lit with candles, to entertain the tenantry, or rather the lawyers and surveyors and businesspeople who had replaced them in the houses and cottages the estate had sold off. Miss Wood LRAM, doyenne of the Braunstonbury Music Society, was in charge of the concert, and while rigorous with regard to repertoire, she was relaxed with regard to recruitment, so an ambitious programme was not always fulfilled thanks to the very mixed ability of her players and singers. It was an especially taxing 'We Three Kings' that had erased what shreds of seasonal goodwill Jane had managed to muster. There had been a stand-off between congregation and performers when they got to the *O-oh* preceding the chorus, which Miss Wood, quite properly, took without any *rallentando*, but for which the congregation slowed down in one of those few moments when it can seize control from the conductor, so the tempo was lost and the

Star of Wonder tumbled across the Bethlehem sky like a satellite knocked out of orbit.

'I enjoyed it,' said Victor, 'it reminded me of . . . I don't know . . . Manderley?'

'I hope not,' said Honoria. 'Manderley burnt down.'

'I mean the Englishness,' he said, 'carols and Christmas trees and tradition. I love that.'

'You don't have Christmas in New York?' said Honoria.

'Of course,' he said, 'but Thanksgiving kind of anticipates it.'

'Fifth Avenue was crawling with Santas last time I looked,' said Jane.

'Oh, sure, but it's not just Christmas, it's Hanukkah, it's Kwanzaa – you know about Kwanzaa?'

'Never heard of it,' said Bernard.

'It's like Christmas for black folks. They light candles, they give gifts, they dress up, they feast. My point is everyone has a different celebration, but we all do Thanksgiving, gathering our families, offering blessings, eating turkey . . .'

'And pumpkin pie,' said Jane, 'one of the more revolting delicacies of my adopted land.'

'But it's tradition,' said Victor, 'like mince pies and that terrible rotten cheese you all have.'

'Tradition, tradition, tradition,' said Jane, looking around the room at the painted shorthorns staring at her from their gilded frames. 'You know what I like about America? It looks forwards, not backwards.'

Honoria could see her father's mood darkening at his cousin's failure of dutifulness and gratitude, and to avoid a scene – there had been so many lately – she put into action a plan to dilute his misanthropy, produce some diversion for their guests and if not raise the spirit of Christmas past, at least blow on its embers.

After breakfast she called the rectory, saying she knew it was last minute, but would Audrey and Daniel like to join them for Christmas lunch at the big house? Audrey said yes at once, because, as Honoria had anticipated, it would take an earthquake to make her decline an invitation to Champton House, but Theo, her other son, was staying, so could she bring him too? Of course she could, they would be delighted.

Audrey replaced the receiver, and the smile she adopted even for telephone conversations with her grand neighbours suddenly relaxed. She bit her lip, wondering what she would do with the provisions she had laid on for the Christmas they had planned, lest they go to waste – unthinkable. And there was another problem, a more difficult problem, about which she resolved to seek the counsel of her son.

The dogs skidded into the rectory kitchen and Daniel closed the door. It resisted a little as he pushed, as if the cold morning air was making a concentrated effort to get in, like a desperate door-to-door salesman. 'What's the emergency?' he said, 'and why so hush-hush?'

'I couldn't say anything in front of your police-man,' said Audrey, nimbly refastening the pinny round her middle. She had always been nimbler than she looked, through force of will rather than natural aptitude, and when she had a project, she set to it with energy and purpose. She was never nimbler than at Christmas, which she went at like a general on campaign, and liked nothing more than the eve of battle, when she reminded him of Henry V at Agincourt anticipating the Feast of Crispin.

The kitchen table was covered with mince-pie tins, each containing a double row of pale pastry dimples. A large Mason Cash mixing bowl, its white inner glaze slightly crazed, was almost full with mince-pie filling so stiff the wooden spoon stood rigidly in it but at an angle, like a mast on a Loch Fyne skiff. In a box in the scullery, Audrey had hidden the jars she had decanted it from, bought from the cash and carry via Jean Shorely, for she was of an age where the labour that went into mincemeat preparation from scratch was no longer worth the result, but she saw no need for anyone else to know. Same with marmalade, and she remembered being caught red-handed by Stella Harper at the cash and carry tills with two giant tins of Robertson's Seville orange mix. Stella's twisted smile of triumph died the moment she remembered that she had the same in her trolley too.

Audrey started to fill each dimple with a dollop of mincemeat.

'Good news or bad news?' she said.

'Good first, please.'

'We've been invited to the big house for Christmas lunch.'

'When?'

'Christmas Day, Daniel. Or did she say Derby Day? I can't remember.'

'I meant, when did the invitation come?'

'Just now.'

'Bit late,' said Daniel.

'Yes, especially when I've got everything in for ours.'

'I wonder why . . .'

'I can tell you exactly why. Jean says they've got Bernard's cousin and her awful husband from America staying and Honoria reckons that's a lump she'll want to leaven, and the leaven is us.'

'Oh dear,' said Daniel. 'I suppose we could do drinks.'

'I've accepted.'

'For lunch?'

'Of course,' said Audrey. 'Christmas lunch at Champton House? There's no higher prize. The whole village will go as green as the holly and the ivy.'

'Hang on,' said Daniel, 'what about . . .?'

'Theo's invited too.'

He made an awkward face. 'But I've just invited Neil to ours for lunch.'

'Oh, have you? Thanks for asking me first. Now you'll have to uninvite him.'

'I can't uninvite him, Mum. He's on his own.'

'Since when has it been your responsibility to take in every waif and stray?'

'It is my responsibility.'

'At *Christmas*?'

'Especially at Christmas.'

Audrey started to stir the stiff mincemeat in a pointless labour that Daniel knew was a pretext to gather her thoughts.

'And the bad news?' he asked.

She stopped stirring. 'I invited Miss March to ours too.'

'Oh,' said Daniel, 'why did you do that?'

'She's on her own too.'

Daniel thought for a moment. 'I wonder if she might be the sort of person who prefers to be alone at Christmas.'

'Nonsense,' said Audrey, 'no one wants to be on their own at Christmas. And besides, there's an Aquascutum suit like that one Mrs Thatcher wore to meet Mr Gorbachev in the window at Elite Fashions and housekeeping won't stretch to that without a discount.'

'Can't you ask Honoria if we could bring Neil and Miss March?'

'I don't think so, dear.'

'Why not?'

Audrey raised an eyebrow.

'What does that mean?' Daniel asked.

'Policemen and shopkeepers? In the state dining room?'

'Oh, Mum, no one cares about that now!'

'I think you'll find they do.' She started spooning mincemeat into pastry cases again.

After a while Daniel said, 'We're going to have to

disappoint Honoria. There's no other way.'

Audrey with a floured finger carefully man-oeuvred a dollop of mincemeat to the very end of the spoon. 'If you think I'm going to cancel Christmas lunch at Champton House, think again.' She gave a little push and it plopped into the pastry case. She considered it, her head at an angle. 'I suppose we couldn't come down with a cold and stand Miss March and your policeman down?'

'I'm presiding at Midnight Mass and on Christmas morning. The whole parish will be there.'

'Colds can strike swiftly. And then a miraculous recovery before luncheon, which they need not know anything about.'

'All Champton would know about it before the flames on the pudding were out.'

Audrey had to concede this was true. 'What about a pastoral emergency?'

'That covers me, but not you. And I'm not lying to get you out of your mess.'

'And yours.'

In Main Street, Miss March was opening Elite Fash-ions. She switched on the Christmas lights in the windows and awaited the rush. It had been a good couple of weeks, as the ladies of Champton and the

Badsaddles splashed out on their Christmas outfits. Today, she thought, would be her best, and she replenished the bales of scarves on the shelves and piles of gloves on the table near the entrance for the last-minute purchases for aunts you had forgotten you had invited, or late additions to the dining table, or for the people you thought just might bring a present even though you had made it clear presents were not expected, and – for one or two of her customers – presents given in the expectation that they would not be reciprocated, which would allow them the quiet pleasure of making someone feel bad.

An imbalance of generosity was a predicament Miss March would very much prefer to avoid. As she checked the till, she frowned at having been forced into exactly that predicament by Audrey Clement.

'I won't *hear* of it,' Mrs Clement had said, with her peculiar habit of emphasising the wrong word, when she had tried to duck the invitation of Christmas lunch at the rectory. It was not that Miss March disliked the prospect of the company or the menu, for the Clements were civilised and Audrey an excellent cook; it was partly that she had planned her day – church in the morning, a slice of ham or something for lunch, the Queen, a nap, then *It'll Be Alright on the Night* with a Marks & Spencer macaroni cheese on a tray. Also, she had been in retail long enough to know the ways of women and had noticed Audrey's calculating eye resting for a moment on the hounds-tooth-check wool suit in the window. Miss March did not easily give a discount, and she knew Audrey would not be so vulgar as to ask, but tasting the rectory marzipan would mean 15 per cent off, she supposed. Then again, it was Christmas, a time for giving, and if it is indeed more blessed to give than to receive then perhaps it would be to her profit, after all.

On the counter lay a pile of woollen gloves – actually quite nice – two serviceable woollen scarves, some sheets of tissue, a length of ribbon, scissors, Sellotape and some tartan wrapping paper in Christmassy colours of red and green and gold.

Miss March started to wrap the first Christmas presents she had given since her father died.

Chapter Two

The stable at Bethlehem was unusually thronged for the Nativity, for there were more children in Champton than parts in the drama, and some had to share their part with another, or sometimes two others. There were two Marys – it had started to get a bit *All About Eve* in the choir vestry – and two Josephs this year, hordes of angels and shepherds and farmyard animals, and the three kings had been joined by a fourth, who had presented himself for duty dressed in his Darth Vader costume and carrying a lightsabre.

But there was something about the towel head-dresses and stick-on beards and tinsel halos that Daniel found affecting – more affecting as he got older. When he was younger and full of zeal he would have pulled a face at 'Away in a Manger', for its sentimentality and poor phrasing, but now he found it poignant – something to do with child-hood perceived from age, he supposed – or he did until they got to the *likkle law Jee-sah*, which almost brought him to tears in a different way.

His brother, too, presented challenges. Theo was an actor, quite well known now, and for that reason when he spent Christmas at Champton he liked to offer his services as narrator for the Nativity, a duty he discharged with a gusto that Daniel quiet-ly found irritating. He read the Bible like one of Shakespeare's racier sonnets, perhaps too alive to the peculiar music and novel energy of Jacobean Eng-lish when Scripture is better read for clarity rather than feeling – whenever it is read. One year he had declaimed the prophetic words of John the Baptist with such portentous force that the arrival of God incarnate had felt like an anti-climax.

This afternoon he got off to a flying start, stirring the cast so much that the angel Gabriel appeared to Mary with a star jump and an expression of shocked surprise that made Daniel think of Hylda Baker. Each Mary found it difficult to release their infant son to the other, one of the shepherds cried because he wasn't allowed an Easter egg, and there were so many animals crammed into the stable – among them bears, ducks, leopards and dolphins – that they started to look like they had strayed into the wrong tableau and should be embarking onto Noah's ark instead.

But was this not Noah's ark reprised? thought Daniel at his most parsonical, or most desperate to find a fresh way into a sermon he had preached so often; is not all creation in that stable saved again from darkness and desolation? Then Melchior was sick down his beard, so Audrey removed him from the narrative and handed him over to his nana, which she pronounced to rhyme with banana.

Miss March's nose wrinkled at this unfortunate expulsion. It had wrinkled several times already, mostly at the behaviour of the adults, who sat at the back of the church, as custom required, but then found themselves too distant from their children when they appeared in role, and obstructed other parents' views of their children by rushing to the front to wave at them and give them reassuring praise. One dad had a little video camera and set about recording the event with the single-minded commitment of Robert Capa at the Normandy landings. The three kings, plus Darth Vader, on their arrival had to step around him as he lay in the aisle for the shot and Theo, seeing this from the lectern, paused the narrative to scold him and then gave a little speech about an audience's obligation to respect the performers and their '*literally* sacred' enactment of the greatest story of all.

And then, after the comedy and chaos, all were assembled in the stable and it was suddenly still. Miss March felt a tear in the corner of her eye and firmly composed herself. Why did this so affect her? Because we were all children once, she thought, stood with tinsel halos, wide-eyed on the edge of a mystery that was still there in adulthood, only smaller and further away. Then they all sang 'Silent Night' with Katrina Gauchet on the guitar and a verse played approximately on whistling recorders and Miss March was quite recovered after that.

Daniel gave the blessing.

> 'May the joy of the angels,
> the delight of the shepherds,
> the perseverance of the kings,
> the patience of Joseph and Mary,
> and the peace of the Christ child
> be yours this Christmas and always.'

'Amen,' the regulars replied, while the parents scrambled for hats and coats and pushchairs and Daniel had to, if not race, then rush out of the vestry door and round the outside of the church so he would be at the porch in time to say goodbye to the departing children and their parents and wish them a merry Christmas. He did this with such expediency that they often looked surprised to see him there, as if he had suddenly bilocated.

His mother and his brother came to stand with him, replicating the de Floures family parade at the carol concert. 'Goodbye, merry Christmas!' said Daniel, swathed in his cloak so he did not have to shake hands with anyone and be infected with the Christmas cold that fells less experienced clergy. He was spared some of that risk by Theo, rather a draw with the adults because of his small but recurring role as PC Henry Heseltine in the daytime soap *Appletree End*, and with the children because of his appearance in an advertisement gurning at a cartoon character over a bowl of breakfast cereal so lively with additives it was reputed to melt spoons. He started to flag after half a dozen handshakes, did a sort of pantomime shrug to indicate he had to be elsewhere, and disappeared. Audrey was of stronger mettle, smiling politely at the mums and nanas, but chatting only to her friends with an incline of the head that she had unconsciously picked up from the Queen Mother.

She was looking over the shoulder of a lady trying to speak to her for someone she liked when her smile froze. 'A *very* merry Christmas,' she interrupted, then she peeled away and took off up the path that led through the churchyard to the rectory. What had necessitated that urgent departure? Daniel wondered, and then looked the other way and understood. Miss March was at the back of the queue waiting to leave and Audrey had evidently decided that if an awkward conversation were to be had, it wouldn't be her having it. Daniel did not panic, or did not appear to, for it would not serve as the still centre of a turning world to waver, but he could not see a way to avoid embarrassment, from either a failure of generosity or truthfulness. Fortunately there was a crowd of people in front of Miss March, all trying to leave, and an observer might have thought the rector unusually fulsome with his Christmas greetings under that pressure, but Daniel calculated that the longer he took, the likelier it would be for those at the back to tire and sneak out through the tower door, like bellringers disinclined to stay for the service they had summoned the faithful to attend.

'And your father ...? Are your grandchildren with you this Christmas ...? Midnight Mass is at half past eleven, but I suggest you get here in good time . . . What a splendid jumper!'

But Miss March valued the virtues of patience and steadfastness and would endure the wait, however long, so that form could be observed and business resolved.

'Yes, it's a busy couple of days . . . Not quite a white Christmas, but you know, "*He giveth snow like wool and scattereth the hoarfrost like ashes . . .*" Have you come far . . .?'

The sweet, spicy odour of mulled wine was beginning to fade as the urns cooled and there came the unmistakable sound of church ladies rustling black binbags – closing time – but still Miss March queued, getting ever nearer. For Daniel, inspiration was still some distance away, nowhere to be seen in fact, and when she finally arrived in front of him he realised he was going to have to do the parson's equivalent of pressing the red button; he was going to have to tell the truth.

'Rector,' she said, 'such a lovely service. I was quite transported back to childhood.'

'Yes, nothing else comes near, don't you find?'

'I do . . .'

'It's the innocence, isn't it? Undimmed by experience?'

'I suppose so. And the carols.'

'Also untouched by experience,' he said.

'Yes, Mrs Gauchet unfailingly encourages the children to sing out. No wonder the baby awakes. But I wanted to ask you about tomorrow.'

'Oh, yes?'

'Can I bring anything?' Miss March asked.

'Bring anything?'

'Yes, for lunch. I have no doubt your mother has it firmly under control, but I have . . . oh, you know, dates, nuts, glacé fruits, that sort of thing . . . I'd offer to do the gravy or the brandy butter but I'm no cook and your mother most certainly is. Is there anything?'

Daniel took a breath. 'Um . . . there is something.'

And suddenly Audrey was there, slightly flushed, for she had run from the rectory the moment she had put the phone down.

'Miss March!'

'Mrs Clement, I was just asking the rector if there's anything I can bring tomorrow.'

'No, only yourself. But it will all be a bit improvised.'

Improvised? thought Daniel; his mother would never improvise Christmas lunch . . .

'We're going to be a larger party than we thought

– all very last minute, but Jean Shorely's been called away to her sister's in Eastbourne – heart attack, or shingles, something – I just spoke to Honoria, and Champton House is without a cook, so I insisted they all come to us.'

'All of them?' said Daniel.

'Yes, of course, we've plenty of room.'

'How many?'

'Lord de Floures, Alex and Honoria, and his cousin and her husband. Only five.'

'Which makes us . . . ten altogether.'

'We can get twenty round our table.'

'The turkey,' said Daniel, 'it won't stretch to ten.'

'Oh,' said Miss March, 'that changes things. Are you going to be overwhelmed? I can easily sit this one out, I quite understand.' There was something in the way she said it that made Daniel think she understood very well how these things went.

'Nonsense!' said Audrey. 'There's plenty; they're having venison anyway – de Floures tradition, apparently – so they'll bring that and our turkey will easily feed eight. And Jean's done a pudding and prepped everything that can be prepped, so it's simply a matter of pooling our sprouts, if you see what I mean.'

'I wonder if it wouldn't be better if I bowed out . . .' said Miss March.

'Unthinkable,' said Audrey. 'I couldn't live with myself to think of you alone on Christmas Day.'

Daniel smiled.

'But it would not bother me at all …' said Miss March. She would much prefer it, in fact, and had Audrey been capable of imagining that this nobly augmented luncheon might not appeal to others as irresistibly as it appealed to her, she might have given her a pass, but she was not.

'An invitation is an invitation,' Audrey pronounced, 'and can no more be revoked than the Ten Commandments.'

'Like thou shalt not bear false witness …' said Daniel.

'So we will see you at half past twelve?'

Miss March nodded. 'Are you quite sure there is nothing I can bring? I can always pop into the Bejam at Braunstonbury if it's open today and get a couple of boxes of pigs-in-blankets.'

'Quite, *quite* sure,' said Audrey. 'See you to-morrow!'

'Tonight, if you're at Midnight Mass?'

'*À bientôt!*'

Miss March walked down the churchyard path in the dying light. She was frowning, not so much at the thought of having to negotiate the social pitfalls of Christmas with strangers, made more perilous by the addition of aristocracy, but more at having to find and wrap five more presents. But at least you can't go wrong with gloves and scarves, she thought.

'Oh, this is simply *too* much,' said Audrey. 'Christmas Eve and we've double numbers for lunch tomorrow . . .'

'Your idea,' said Daniel, 'so don't complain,' though he knew that complaining about a predicament she had engineered herself was half the fun.

'Must you invite *every* waif and stray, Daniel?'

'Neil. I invited Neil. You've invited half the county.'

But Audrey wasn't listening. 'Theo . . .'

Her son had been cutting crosses into a pile of Brussels sprouts – a pointless exercise he suspected, needless effort for a loveless vegetable, but a ritual is a ritual.

'. . . you must liaise with Honoria and fetch whatever needs to be fetched from the big house. But not everything tonight; they can leave stuff in their fridge and the cold room until tomorrow morning, when it's needed . . .'

'Do you want me to do that now?'

Audrey ignored him, tore two sheets of lined

paper out of her kitchen notebook and scrunched them up. 'We need a *whole* new plan.' She sat down at the kitchen table. 'Sit, sit, sit!'

Theo and Daniel sat.

She took a pencil from her pinny pocket and wrote in capital letters 'REVISED CHRISTMAS PLAN' at the top of a fresh sheet.

'Christmas Eve,' she said out loud as she wrote, 'prep veg ... Theo's on sprouts and carrots; Dan, you're on parsnips and potatoes ...'

'I have to take Holy Communion to Canon Dolben at Pitcote before Midnight Mass, so I may have to leave you to it ...'

'Oh, blast,' said Audrey. 'Can't he do it himself?'

'He's ninety, Mum, and he's on his own in an old folks' home.'

'Don't make it unnecessarily long, you don't want to tire him out. And don't start doling out communion to the others ... You can lay the table. We're ten. Have we got enough of everything for ten? I think we've only got eight of best.'

'Then we'll have to mix and match,' said Theo.

'They'll think us *savages* ...'

'They won't,' he said.

'WINE, what about WINE?'

'I'm sure—'

'CRACKERS! Box of six, that's all we've got. What are we going to do? Will they bring their own? What if their crackers are more splendid than ours? They couldn't be less splendid – I got them from the cash and carry.'

'I don't think they do crackers,' said Daniel, 'and if they did, they wouldn't get them from Asprey's.'

'Dan, that's a job for you: stop off in Braunston-bury on the way to Pitcote, and get another box, cheap and cheerful!'

'Will anywhere be open?'

'Of course it will, it's Christmas bloody Eve.'

Headlights flickered outside and then came the sound of tyres on the gravel. There was a knock at the back door and the dogs hurled themselves at it, barking. It was Bernard, who fussed over the dogs, ignored Theo and Daniel, and spoke to Audrey.

'Dear lady,' he said, 'Honoria tells me you have saved the day – so kind of you . . .'

'Come in, come in,' said Audrey, patting down her pinny in the manner of Mrs Bridges from *Upstairs Downstairs*, which she did not mean to do but could not help it.

'I bring gifts,' he said, then looked at Daniel and Theo, 'if you could give me a hand?'

They returned with gifts indeed, half a dozen bottles of white burgundy, half a dozen of claret and a whole Stilton so *à point* it seemed almost to glow in the dark. A handsome dole, thought Daniel, but not quite the Puligny-Montrachet and Romanée-St-Vivant he knew Bernard kept in his cellar for a more favoured few.

'I'm beverages but Honoria is in charge of edibles,' said Bernard, 'so you'll need to speak to her about that.'

'So kind,' said Audrey, 'but how is poor Jean, or poor Jean's sister?'

'Heart attack or a stroke or something, not sure. Very sad. She has no one so Mrs Shorely has had to fly to her bedside. Can't be helped. So we are really most grateful . . .'

'Not at all, not at all,' said Audrey, in one of those self-deprecating phrases English people use in response to something that has not actually been said, 'we're delighted to have you all with us.'

'You say that *now*,' said Bernard, 'but you don't really know my cousin and her husband.'

'I think we met before,' said Audrey, 'was it three Christmases ago?'

'He's fussy, like so many Americans. Wants constant attention. Can't eat anything or drink anything, doctor's orders, or so he says. She's been in New York so long she's gone native, but I think at heart she knows it's all nonsense.'

'Fussy eater? What sort of things won't he eat?'

'Oh, don't worry about that. Give him a plate of sprouts if he's tricky, he's used to it.'

'What about her?'

'Cousin Jane? I don't think I've ever known her turn down a free feed.'

'But she's so thin!'

'I don't think she really likes *eating*. It's being given things that she likes. I remember her last husband, before she reduced him to beggary, saying the Nizam of Hyderabad couldn't keep her in diamonds. God knows how Victor manages. But how ungallant of me to speak of her this way. Is there anything else I can bring?'

'I'll talk to Honoria,' said Audrey.

'I should. See you tomorrow.'

'Not at Midnight Mass?' she asked.

'God, no. I'm not a Moonie,' and he left.

'What did he mean by that?' said Theo.

'Bernard doesn't like enthusiasm in church,' said Daniel. 'He's down-the-line Book of Common Prayer, Sunday morning, no new hymns and a five-minute sermon. Nothing fancy.'

Audrey said, 'I agree. Church should be done plainly and always the same.'

'Except at Christmas,' said Daniel.

'No, especially at Christmas. I want it just the same as always. Mary and Joseph. Angels. Descants. Gold, frankincense and myrrh.'

'It may be the same, but it isn't plain,' said Daniel. 'Because everyone's High Church at Christmas. The Virgin Mary centre stage. Twinkling lights. Incense.'

'Oh, yes,' said Audrey, 'the incense. It seems such a shame to smoke us out, even if it is only once a year. But why Christmas? For lots of people it's the only time they're in church and you turn it into a kasbah.'

'Frankincense.'

'What about it?'

'Incense. It "owns a deity nigh". You sing it, loudly, every year in "We Three Kings".'

Audrey thought about it for a moment. 'I also sing about lords a-leaping, drummers drumming and a partridge in a pear tree, and where are they? If you laid them on it would cause a *sensation*.'

There were more headlights, then another knock at the door. The dogs, who had retreated to their bed by the Aga, hurled themselves at it again. It was Alex de Floures, Bernard's second son and least favourite child, accompanied by Nathan Liversedge, the old gamekeeper's grandson, who had graduated from his mean employment and lived scandalously with Alex in the lodge houses on either side of the park gates.

'What did Daddy want?' said Alex.

'Wine and cheese delivery,' said Theo.

Alex looked in the boxes. 'Hmm,' he said.

'I cut some mistletoe in the old orchard, Mrs Clement,' said Nathan. 'Thought you might like some.'

'Mistletoe!' said Audrey. 'Haven't had any in years! Thank you!'

He went to the car and brought in a tangle of the pale-green parasite with its pearly berries that clustered in the branches of Champton's apple trees, no longer carefully tended.

'Where do you want it?'

'Hanging from the main light in the hall, I think. Theo, fetch the stepladder.'

Nathan separated a bunch from the tangle, cut a length of string from his pocket with a knife, and in one of those unconscious acknowledgements of ceremony they all watched while he climbed the stepladder and tied it to the bottom of the large lantern light in the hall.

'So pretty,' said Audrey.

'So pagan,' said Alex. 'Wasn't it something to do with druids?'

'Celts, certainly,' said Daniel. 'A fertility symbol. Not just the Celts, the Greeks too. They called it oak sperm.'

'When I was a girl we called it the Kissing Bough,' said Audrey, 'which I think we would all prefer.'

'I've got holly too,' said Nathan. 'Would you like some of that?'

'You are so kind,' said Audrey.

They laid holly along the tops of the pictures in the drawing room, and along the chimney piece there and in the dining room, Audrey impatiently collecting the Christmas cards that she had put up there because she had a faint feeling that Christmas cards were vulgar and greenery was smart. The vulgarity did not usually bother her because she and Daniel received so many cards – parsons always do – and it seemed to her a blazon of popularity to strew them on every flat surface. But tomorrow they would be hosting Lord de Floures and his family, and she would not want them to think her vulgar. Last, they laid holly across the tops of the portraits of Daniel's predecessors hanging in the hall. Theo switched on the lantern so the mistletoe cast its shadows across the walls and the black-and-white flagged floor and they stood back and admired the intrusion of forestry into the rectory's sleek geometry, which made Audrey think for a moment of mould advancing on a block of supermarket Cheddar.

> 'All the sleepy dancers gone,
> Just one candle burning on,
> Shadows lurking everywhere:
> Some one came, and kissed me there.'

'What's that, Daniel?' said Alex.
'It's "Mistletoe". Walter de la Mare.'
He grimaced. 'Creepy.'

Chapter Three

'I'm sure you've noticed that the season of peace and goodwill, in spite of our best intentions, conspires to erode both, and if we're not careful it can degenerate into the kind of battle zone the unfortunate residents of Walford entertain us with year by year.'

Daniel in the pulpit looked round the church at faces, softened by candlelight, looking back at him with the faint curiosity so familiar to preachers at Midnight Mass. He had hoped his reference to *EastEnders*, which Audrey had become secretly addicted to since Dirty Den served divorce papers on the faithless Ange amid the tinsel of a cheerless Yule, would provoke a flicker of interest, but it did not.

'I sometimes think *EastEnders*' Christmases are so miserable in order to neutralise our own feelings of animosity as stress builds up. If they're having a punch-up in the Queen Vic, or throwing presents at each other round the Christmas tree, then we don't have to.

'Was it ever thus? Well, imagine what it was like a lifetime ago for men returning to Champton from northern France and Belgium and Gallipoli and Palestine, after four years of the bloodiest war the world had ever seen. Some of you don't have to imagine it, because you will remember it – just. How did carols proclaiming peace on Earth and goodwill to all men sound then? Or go back another few lifetimes, to when the king's men were defeated by Cromwell at Naseby, and Royalists and Parliamentarians, sometimes from the same family – some from Champton – slew each other in the fields and woods where we walk today.

'I heard someone on the news suggest that we are divided now as bitterly as we were back then. An exaggeration, but we are hardly at peace with ourselves, disagreeing about matters of fundamental importance, with the profitability of businesses and the livelihoods of workers at stake. No wonder Christmas at the Queen Vic feels so compelling.

'And in the middle of this, we look up, to see a

star over a pub, in an insignificant place, and a baby in a manger, tiny and vulnerable.

'Two thousand years ago Israel looked for a war-rior king to deliver it from enslavement; in 1649 our ancestors cut off the king's head and proclaimed a new dawn; in 1918, back from the battlefields, they looked for a world beyond war.

'And what came was a baby, in a manger, tiny and vulnerable.

'Tiny and vulnerable – but an answer, once and for all, to the sum of human stupidity and strife. Not a warrior, or a buccaneer, or a boffin, but one who surrenders to the worst we have to offer and, to the amazement of all generations, turns darkness into light, despair into hope, the prison of the past into a limitless future.

'Do you remember the Christmases of childhood? I think you do, like me, because why else be here? If that's what stirred you tonight to come to church, and hear again the message of the angels, and maybe bang out "Hark the Herald . . ." one more time, I suggest that's not simply nostalgia, or whimsy, or an effort to please; it's because in the deepest night we see that light shining still, and it reveals the path which leads us with the shepherds, and the wise men, and our numberless ancestors, to peace and joy.

'May that light burn brightly for you and those you love, and a happy and holy Christmas to all. Amen.'

'Amen,' replied the churchy people; the others mumbled something and looked around to see if they were supposed to stand up or sing something.

Daniel descended from the pulpit and went to sit in the celebrant's chair, flanked by the junior servers, Scott and Matthew Harleston. Scott was too old now for this kind of thing, and his cassock was six inches too short, but still he volunteered for Christmas. His brother was too young really to be allowed up this late, but he had been for this most special occasion, and was also young enough not to mask his excitement. They kept a few moments of silence after the sermon, so that the preacher's words might take root, but nobody was thinking about the sermon except the preacher.

Matthew started to fidget. Daniel got to his feet. 'We stand and say together the Creed. You will find the words in bold type in your service booklet ... "*We believe in one God, the Father, the Almighty ...*"'

After the service Daniel stood at the door in his cloak shaking hundreds of hands and saying

'Happy Christmas' so many times the words began to detach from their meaning, and by the end the vowels were in the right order but the consonants were jumbled, not that anyone seemed to mind or notice.

One of the last to appear out of the shadows was Victor.

'Hello,' said Daniel. 'I didn't see that you were here. Are you on your own?'

'I am. Too late for Jane. And Bunny.'

'The de Floures genes are not noted for producing an inexhaustible appetite for worship.'

'I guess not,' said Victor.

'But you?'

'I find it fascinating, what you do here.'

'I have never spent a Christmas in America, so I don't know what you are used to.'

'I'm not sure I could tell you. My religious commitment was nominal. Not a big thing for us. Not until recently.'

'It has changed?'

'Yes. As I've got older, I've got more curious about . . . faith.'

Daniel slightly braced himself for the kind of conversation people who have recently got curious about faith like to have.

'It struck me', said Victor, 'that the faith of my forefathers, and foremothers, was so important to them they crossed an ocean with nothing, to find a new life in a new world. That's something, isn't it?'

'I used to preach from a pulpit', said Daniel, 'where the vicar in the seventeenth century persuaded his flock to do precisely that. And they bundled up what they could take with them, boarded a leaky wooden ship, and sailed through storms and tempests to what we now call Massachusetts. Like your ancestors?'

'We ended up in New York,' said Victor, 'though it was New Amsterdam before it was New York. As you get older you also get more interested in where you come from, who you are. Americans especially, because we're all from somewhere else. So I got more curious about them, and that meant getting more curious about faith. It fascinates me.'

'Historical interest?'

'At first, but then I found I wanted to participate. So I do now, quietly. But, seriously, it's ... I guess you will have heard this before ... it's like I opened a door and walked into a room that was always there, waiting for me. And it's my room and I must try to live in it. I'm not explaining this well.'

46

'I think you explain it very well,' said Daniel.

'I'd love to talk it through with you sometime, if we get the chance. It's not something I can talk about much. Jane doesn't like it. She thinks it's like golf.'

'Golf?'

'Yes, something husbands abandon their wives for.'

Daniel smiled. 'There are worse things you can abandon a wife for.'

'Not as far as Jane's concerned. But I try to keep her happy. She's coming in the morning. Bunny kind of insisted.'

'I'll see you then. Perhaps we can find some time to talk tomorrow.'

'Maybe. Thanks. And goodnight.'

Victor, followed by the last of the midnight worshippers, disappeared down the path, and then only Neil was left.

'Happy Christmas,' he said after Daniel had closed and bolted the big south door.

'Same to you, Neil. Thanks for your help. But don't you want to get home? It's nearer one than midnight.'

'I'll give you a hand. What needs to be done? I've put out all the candles and collected the service books. They're on the table.'

'I've just got to fill in the register and set up the altar.'

They walked up the aisle towards the chancel and the priests' vestry. The smell of burnt incense and snuffed candles hung in the air.

'What do you want to do with this one?' Neil pointed towards the Nativity, where a single light in a glass burnt in front of the manger where the bambino now lay.

'Why didn't you blow it out?'

'I thought it might be one of those eternal flames, like the one in front of the box where you keep Holy Communion.'

'Your instinct was right,' said Daniel. 'We leave a light burning at the crib from Midnight Mass until the three kings come.'

They carried on under the chancel arch and into the vestry, where Daniel opened the register and started to fill in the figures. 'How many do you think we had in tonight, Neil?'

'Must have been a hundred and fifty?'

'One hundred and forty-four,' Daniel said, writing the figure into the relevant column.

'Is that your imagination activated?'

'It's not a *precise* science. And of those hundred and forty-four, how many received communion? About

48

ninety? I counted out a hundred and fifty wafers and there were more than fifty left. Not that long ago everyone would have received communion.'

'What happened?'

'It just started to . . . fade. Would you mind hanging up those cassocks and cottas?' Scott and Matthew had left their vesture in heaps on the floor.

'That's what I thought the Second Advent would look like when I was a boy,' said Neil, 'our clothes left in a pile behind us when Jesus took us up to heaven. Embarrassing, floating up with the choir ladies all in the nude.'

As Neil hung up the cassocks and cottas, Daniel refilled two glass jugs with water and wine, and then took the lid off a large silver vessel and started filling it with wafers, which came in a row of a hundred wrapped in cellophane. 'Won't be so many tomorrow morning, eighty at most at the main service. And maybe forty at the earlier one, I think.' He filled a smaller silver lidded vessel. 'Could you take those chalices and the ciboriums and put them on the altar? The cups with the lid?'

Daniel joined Neil at the altar and laid everything out with the neat precision that came with years of practice. He finished by holding the heavily embroidered veil over the vessels and then dropping it so it fell over them to form an almost perfect symmetrical shape. He pinched the front corners to make it tidy and laid the burse, a sort of square embroidered wallet containing a crisp white linen cloth, on top. 'Done,' he said.

'When's your first service?' said Neil.

'Eight. Then the ten-thirty.'

'It's a long haul, isn't it?'

'Tomorrow's not so bad, only two services, but that's on top of no sleep, the carol services, the home communions, things in school, the big services in church and the call-outs. But I haven't had a call-out this Christmas. Not so far.'

'What sort of thing?'

'Deathbeds. Can't remember the last Christmas I didn't have one. Mortality rates go up in December and January.'

'So do murders.'

'There you go.'

'And you've got a houseful for Christmas dinner as well,' Neil pointed out.

'Mum and Theo are taking care of that.'

'Won't you be knackered?'

'Yes. Won't you? It's very late.'

'I'm not on duty. Can I do anything to help tomorrow?'

'I'm sensing we may have to draw on your re-serves of patience. I gather Mr and Mrs Cabot can be testing guests and Bernard in a bad mood is not exactly the Sugar Plum Fairy.'

Neil nodded. 'I wonder how he'll manage being guest, not host.'

'He's always the host in Champton. But that's tomorrow. Do you fancy a nightcap at the rectory?'

'No, I'll let you get to bed. Unless there's anything more you need help with?'

'Don't think so. I'll let you out of the vestry door.'

Outside, a frost had formed that sparkled when Neil switched on his torch.

'Goodnight, Dan,' he said, and set off carefully down the path.

'Goodnight. And happy Christmas.'

'We've done that already,' said Neil, without turning.

Daniel half closed the vestry door but stayed to watch Neil making his way through the churchyard. The torchlight fell across headstones and yews, cast-ing flickering shadows that made Daniel think of ominous carols in minor keys about myrrh and the tomb and the fate of the infant king in the manger, clothed in grave sheets with thorns for a crown. The cold sneaked through the door as he shut it and made him shiver.

He locked up, made his way silently through the churchyard and let himself into the rectory as quietly as he could through the back door, but the dogs barked before he'd even turned the handle. He went to hush them, but the door opened onto a scene busy with industry. Theo was sitting at the kitchen table wrapping presents and Audrey was standing at the counter studding an onion with cloves.

'Oh, bread sauce!' said Daniel.

'Naturally,' said Audrey. 'No bread sauce, no Christmas.'

Every family has its own bespoke delicacy, and for the Clements it was Audrey's bread sauce. It was not one of the mother sauces as defined by Escoffier in *Le guide culinaire* – béchamel, espagnole, tomate, velouté, hollandaise – but it was nectar to them, a rich and creamy confection of breadcrumbs cooked very gently in a bain-marie, with butter and milk and cream and cloves and peppercorns and onions and bay, and an ingredient that was known only to Audrey, which set it apart from lesser bread sauces – an ingredient she flatly refused to share with anyone. Hers was so much better than any other bread sauce Daniel had tasted, and he had tried to make it himself ever since he was a curate, but whenever he asked Audrey for the recipe she just said, 'Oh, just take a bit of this and a bit of that . . .' *A bit of what . . .?* 'Breadcrumbs, milk, an onion . . .' *How long should I cook it for . . .?* 'As long as it takes . . .'

'I wonder if it goes with venison,' she said. 'Do you think I should make a redcurrant gravy as well?'

'Won't Mrs Shorely have made some already?'

'I expect so,' said Audrey and wrinkled her nose.

'Redcurrant gravy *and* cranberry sauce?' said Theo.

'Chalk and cheese!' said Audrey. 'Cranberry sauce with venison doesn't sound right to me at all. Do you think the American will want ketchup? Have we got any? But, darling, hadn't you better get to bed? You have to be up early.'

'Don't *you*?' Daniel asked.

'I'm not going to the eight o'clock.'

'I mean to cook.'

'I've done most of it,' said Audrey. 'The turkey will be two hours in the Aga, Honoria's doing the venison at the big house, drinks at twelve-thirty, lunch at one, Queen at three. Why don't you go to bed?'

Daniel sat at the kitchen table. 'I wouldn't mind a whisky.'

'Theo, get your brother a whisky.'

'There's one in for Christmas,' he said, 'the Macallan, your favourite.'

Theo went out to the drawing room and came back with two tumblers, each with a finger's worth of whisky in them. 'Do you want some soda in this or something, Dan?'

'Just water, please, a splash.'

'I know you'll think me a barbarian, Dan, but I have ice in mine.'

'In the Macallan?'

'Why not? It's just a drop of water in a different form.'

'Doesn't it make it . . . tight?'

'It makes me tight, however I have it,' said Theo.

'No, I mean it shuts down the flavours.'

'I think that's nonsense.'

So there was ice in Theo's, a drop of water in Daniel's, and Audrey decided to have a Noilly Prat because it was Christmas.

'Happy Christmas!' said Daniel.

'I suppose it is, isn't it?' said his mother. 'Happy Christmas!'

The three chinked glasses, although Audrey thought this was common.

Dan said, 'Don't put our presents under the tree. We'll have them later when everyone's gone home. I don't want people to feel embarrassed if they haven't got one or brought one.'

'What about the dogs' presents?' said Theo. 'I've done their stockings.'

'What?' said Audrey.

'I've done their stockings.'

'But they're still awake!'

Chapter Four

Daniel was awake to see Christmas Day dawn. He had got to bed at two and it was now six. Four hours of sleep, and he felt sluggish. He came downstairs, let the dogs out for a pee, and stood at the back door. The light crept up over the horizon and gave a sort of lemony blush to the frost-whitened fields and woods. No snow now, but a white Christmas of sorts, and the church looked so handsome draped in what looked like veils of gauze where powdery hoarfrost had fallen across it. His breath plumed in the freezing air and the dogs were not long on their garden patrol and went straight back to their bed next to the Aga.

The kitchen looked like a church hall taken over by Crisis at Christmas: lidded pots and pans stood on every surface; on the kitchen table there were presents badly wrapped, Theo having gone about that job like a removal man rather than a shop assistant. There were foil-covered trays, bits of torn-off baking parchment on the floor, and in the middle of the kitchen table Audrey's Christmas notebook, wrinkled from years of exposure to spillages, its pages falling out and stuck back in. Somewhere in that, he mused, is her recipe for bread sauce, and he thought for a moment of seeing if he could find it, like Von Tischendorf going through the bundles of manuscripts at the St Catherine's Monastery in Sinai in search of a fourth-century Gospel of Luke. He stopped himself, partly because it would seem slightly dishonest and he did not want to get this high and holy day off to that kind of a start, and partly because the longer he stayed in the kitchen the greater the temptation to help himself to a mince pie – there were dozens of them left to cool in their trays.

He was hungry – he always was when he was busy – but he never ate before the eight o'clock service, maintaining the old discipline of not consuming anything before Holy Communion. It once occurred to him that worrying about the transubstantiated Jesus arriving in his stomach to find a semi-digested boiled egg was a bit peculiar, but he did not give it much thought. That was the point of discipline, to automate routine things, so you could concentrate on the mysterious things.

The mysteries of the eight o'clock Holy Communion were reassuringly sturdy. Bernard, who, if he came to church on a regular Sunday, was more likely to come to the eight o'clock than the ten-thirty, insisted as patron on the use of the Book of Common Prayer – 'If it was good enough for Henry VIII then it's good enough for me,' he said, although it had nothing to do with Henry VIII. Daniel actually used the 1928 revision of the 1662 revision, which was not strictly speaking proper because Parliament had rejected it in one of the more vivid examples of the Church of England trampling its own flowerbeds. Daniel loved it. It retained much of the beauty and mystery of the original but dropped more challenging texts, like 'men's carnal lusts and appetites, like brute beasts that have no understanding', which invariably at weddings provoked blushes, alarm or sniggers depending on the demographic.

These considerations were not in the minds of the small but relentlessly faithful congregation who came to the early service and cost him two hours of precious sleep every Christmas.

'O God our Father, whose Word hath come among us in the Holy Child of Bethlehem: grant that the light of faith may illumine our hearts and shine in all our words and deeds; through him who is Christ the Lord.'

'Amen,' the congregation replied and were out half an hour after they'd arrived without having to sing a single chorus of 'The First Nowell', for the eight o'clock was always said, not sung.

The main service of Holy Communion followed at ten-thirty, the Farmers' Communion, as Daniel called it. It was the tradition in those parts for the farming families to come to church on Christmas Day rather than to Midnight Mass, for in spite of the tradition of the animals being given the power of speech at midnight on Christmas Eve, they could not tell the difference between Christmas Day and the fourteenth Sunday after Trinity, and would need milking and feeding at the usual time. The tradition also required them to dress as only farmers could in their Sunday best, the men in tweed suits under bat-tered Barbours, women in hats and gloves, and their children like miniaturised versions of the parents. It was like the 1950s had come to church.

This was the service Bernard attended too, at Christmas and at Easter, when he was expected to behave seigneurially at the door for tenants and neighbours. The de Floures sat slightly apart in the family pew, with its own door, velvet kneelers and access to the family tombs behind, anticipating a distinction in the afterlife as in this, but if that was the expectation then the first experience of heaven, if achieved, would surely be a disappointment. Daniel had raised this once with Bernard, who testily replied, 'In my Father's house there are many mansions,' as if that were proof from Holy Writ of his rights and privileges enduring into the hereafter.

Today the pew was fuller than usual; Bernard, dressed like a farmer in his Sunday best too, was joined by Honoria in jeans and boots and a cashmere shawl, which made her look glorious, and Alex in jeans and boots and a leather jacket, which made him look Camden Market. Cousin Jane and Victor were there too; she was dressed like Nancy Reagan at Thanksgiving, he in the same tweed suit he had worn yesterday, which looked even more out of place among the farmers because he had tried too hard to look right. That awkwardness was evident again when he tried to join in. He may have started to rediscover the faith of his fathers, but he was still unsure when to stand and when to sit, holding his hymn book upside down and back to front, and singing the 'how silently, how silently' in 'O Little Town of Bethlehem' with a confident *fortissimo* when everyone else went *pianissimo*. He stood when Bernard got up to read the lesson and sat down again in a slightly pantomime way, as if it were something he had intended to do.

In church, Bernard would read only from the Authorised Version and took to the lectern the old Bible he kept in his pew, but when he opened it the slips of paper he had marked his place with fell out, so Daniel had to turn up the passage from Isaiah for him, which made him testy.

'For unto us a child is born, unto us a son is given,' he growled, 'and the government shall be upon his shoulder: and his name shall be called Wonderful, Counsellor, The mighty God, The everlasting Father, The Prince of Peace . . .'

The choir, a little depleted for Christmas for some of them went to relatives elsewhere, attempted for the anthem that very text set by Handel in his *Messiah*; a brave attempt indeed. Margaret Porteous, churchwarden, who volunteered for choir duties on high and holy days, had so enjoyed singing the descant for 'O Come, All Ye Faithful' at Midnight Mass that she went for the high note on 'the mighty GOD' with such uncontrolled energy she was not so much sharp as ballistic, and the stained glass rattled in its panes.

Bernard was normally out of his pew and halfway down the aisle before Jane Thwaite was three bars into the organ voluntary – today a jolly but not taxing piece by Bennett from the green *Old English Organ Music for Manuals* book, the same which she played for Easter, weddings, funerals and Remembrance Sunday too – but at Christmas especially, *noblesse oblige*, so he stood at the door with Daniel wishing parishioners and tenants and neighbours 'a very merry Christmas!' with a sort of bonhomie.

'Happy Christmas, m'lord,' said the older farmers, some of them with grandfathers and great-grandfathers and great-great-grandfathers who had said the same to Bernard's grandfather and great-grandfather and great-great-grandfather before them. 'And to her ladyship,' said one, and then blushed as bright as a holly berry, for her ladyship (Bernard's third) had given up on his lordship years ago and now lived in her native Siena.

The rest of the de Floures party trickled out. Jane felt under no obligation to stay and Victor did not know what they were expected to do, so he took his cue from her and they glided past. 'See you in the library,' Jane said to Bernard, 'if we have time?'

'I think we're expected at the rectory at half past twelve, so enough time for a drink.'

'Shall we walk through the park, Victor?' Jane then asked her husband.

Honoria and Alex lined up next to their father, in order of enthusiasm. How good she is at this sort of thing, thought Daniel, and how bad he is.

'. . . Merry Christmas, and how is your mother . . .?'

'. . . ding dong merrily and all that, yeah . . .'

Bernard, punctilious in this, saw off the last of the farmers, then went back inside to retrieve his gloves from the pew, but was trapped by Margaret Porteous, who thrust a cup of tea on him like a conjuror forcing a card.

'Lord Bernard,' she said, with a look of pantomime concern, 'is Jean *very* upset?'

'Mrs Margaret,' replied Bernard, repeating the solecism in the hope she would stop calling him that, 'you know Mrs Shorely, she just gets on with things.'

'I didn't know she had a sister. Bournemouth?'

'Eastbourne. She keeps a hotel.'

Alex overheard him and said, 'Double toast at table three!' which made his father scowl.

'Was she in service at Champton too?' said Mrs Porteous.

'Years ago, yes. My mother's lady's maid when we had such things. Then the war came, and she got married.'

64

'Will Jean be away long?'

'I couldn't say.'

'Only, if you need any help in the house – entertaining your guests, I mean – I would be more than happy to.'

'So kind, but I think we can manage,' said Bernard.

'Poor Honoria, cooking for you all!'

'We shall be lunching at the rectory. Audrey very generously offered to take us in.'

'Oh,' said Mrs Porteous, unable to keep a note of disappointment out of her voice. 'How fortunate!'

'Yes,' said Bernard, 'we're very grateful,' but Margaret did not mean him.

He handed her the cup of untouched tea and wished her a merry Christmas.

Daniel was talking to Honoria and Alex by the porch. 'Is everything under control?' he asked.

'Yes,' said Honoria, 'the venison's in our Aga – I'll bring it down – the turkey's in yours, there are two puddings steaming, vegetables ready to go, gravy ready to go, and everything else is done, I think. Your mother is being quite mysterious about the bread sauce.'

'A recipe as closely guarded as the formula for Mr Lea and Mr Perrins's Worcestershire Sauce.'

'I can't wait to try it.'

'Such an *English* sort of condiment,' said Alex. 'A sauce made out of bread. *So* Delia.'

'I think it's a hangover from the Middle Ages,' said Daniel, 'when bread was used to thicken sauces. Before we'd heard of roux or anything like that. I love it. It's the taste of home. And Mum does something with hers that elevates it. I don't know what.'

Bernard appeared. 'Shall we go?' he said – it was a command, not a question. 'We'll be with you at half past twelve, Daniel. What's the time now?'

'It's nearly twelve,' said Honoria.

'Why don't you just come to the rectory now?' said Daniel. 'Pointless to go home only to turn round again and come back.'

'I've got to pick up the venison and the pudding,' said Honoria. 'But, Daddy, you don't need to come back.'

'What about Cousin Jane?'

'I can bring Jane and Victor. Can I have the keys to the Land Rover?'

Honoria and Alex got into Bernard's old Land Rover and chugged away down Church Lane.

'They'll be home before Cousin Jane,' said Bernard. 'She's barely had time for a gimlet, or whatever they drink. Are you ready to go?'

'I just have to lock up.'

'Can't Achurch do it?'

'He's already gone.'

'I don't want to be a nuisance, but I *really* don't want to get cornered by Margaret Porteous.'

'Why don't you go over to the rectory? I won't be a minute.'

Bernard nodded and walked down the path that led to the gate in the rectory garden wall. Daniel wondered if he'd go to the back door and walk in without knocking like he still did with tenants, or to the front and ring the bell, so Audrey could admit him into the hall, as she would like to, for she had gone to some effort to smarten it up in the manner she normally only did when the bishop came to tea.

'Rector,' said Margaret, advancing on him from the now-empty church, 'your word, please, on the one-bite mince pies. Yes? Yes?'

Bernard went to the back door. The kitchen windows were steamed up thanks to the battery of pans boiling on the Aga, and it was noisy because Audrey had put the wireless on for *The Archers*. She had all year counted herself an advocate for Ruth and David getting together, even though Ruth was a northerner, and now they were wed she felt as indulgent towards them as a new mother-in-law.

The radio was now playing Christmassy comedy clips, and she had so enjoyed Joyce Grenfell that she was singing 'Stately as a Galleon' and did not see Bernard let himself in. It was only when he wished her a merry Christmas that she turned round from the counter.

'Bernard!' she said crossly. 'Really!' She was not only startled, but disconcerted that his lordship had caught her in the kitchen in her floury pinny and slightly pink from effort.

'Audrey,' he said, unusually defensive, 'Daniel said I could . . .'

Audrey recovered herself. 'I wasn't expecting you for another half an hour! I'm not respectable.'

'I'll just sit in the drawing room quietly until the others arrive. Please don't let me get in your way.'

Audrey wiped her hands on her pinny, embla-zoned with the logo of the Champton and the Badsaddles WI. 'Come through,' she said. 'Theo's in the drawing room . . .'

Theo, who had laid and lit the fire as ordered ten minutes ago, was sitting on the sofa beguiling Cosmo and Hilda with slivers of smoked salmon from the canapés Audrey had unwisely entrusted to his care. They were so beguiled by this, and he by them, that none of them looked up when she and Bernard appeared.

'Theo,' said Audrey, 'would you please take care of Lord de Floures? I'm at a critical stage with lunch.'

'Oh, hello,' said Theo, peering behind him, 'are you alone?'

'I'm early,' said Bernard, 'no point in going home after church if I'm only going to turn round and come straight back again. But I *really* don't want to be a nuisance.'

'We're so glad to have you!' said Audrey and left.

Theo got up from the sofa and presented Bernard with the plate of Audrey's Christmas checkerboard – little squares of buttered brown bread, half of them black, spread with lumpfish roe, the other half red, topped with smoked salmon. Unfortunately, the pattern had been spoiled, for Theo had already helped himself to three. 'Red or black?' he said. 'Oh, that's Stendhal!'

Bernard took one of each.

'And can I get you a drink? Sherry? Henkell Trocken? Shloer?'

Bernard could not help saying, 'What sort of sherry?'

'Croft Original, I think,' said Theo, then he added

in a fruity voice, 'One instinctively knows when something is right . . .'

'What?'

'It's from the advert on telly.'

'I'll take one.'

Theo poured him a glass from the decanter with its engraved little silver gorget. Bernard, who would never have made a spy or a poker player, for he found it almost impossible to dissemble a feeling, raised an eyebrow at the little thimble on a stalk – one of Audrey's cherished sherry glasses, inherited from aunts who had different glasses for everything, from punch to Marsala.

'Don't you do television advertisements?' said Bernard. 'Alex told me you were once a squirrel eating a chocolate bar. Was it a squirrel?'

'Yes,' said Theo, 'at the start of my career, but I was only the voice. I didn't have to dress up as one.'

'And do you do theatre too? Shakespeare, Chekhov, Shaw?'

'Not so much now.'

'Oh, bad luck. I suppose it's an up-and-down sort of living?'

'No, mostly up now. Television, a bit of film.'

'What might I have seen you in?'

'I play a character in a soap opera. On the

television. A policeman. In *Appletree End.*'

Bernard took a sip of sherry. 'I think that's the programme Mrs Shorely likes. But what might *I* have seen you in?'

Miss March was the first to arrive after Bernard. On the very stroke of half past twelve – Audrey heard the quarters chime from the church tower with the peculiar clarity that happens only in very cold, very still weather – the doorbell rang. Theo almost leapt to answer it for his conversation with Bernard had slowed almost to a stall after Bernard had asked him how he managed to learn all those lines when he was in a play.

Under her sensible, well-cut and thrice-reproofed coat, Miss March was dressed as she was always dressed, soberly, in a grey tweed suit from Harvey Nichols and a white blouse, and shod in black Bally court shoes with little golden buckles. In a concession to the gaiety of the season she wore on her lapel a little holly-shaped brooch in gold with green enamel and a cluster of rubies for berries. Miss March did not have wardrobes of outfits, racks of shoes and coffers of jewels, but what she had was the best she could afford, sometimes a little more than she could afford, partly because she had been in retail all her adult life, selling shoes to the better class of person in the cathedral city of Stow and dresses to the better class of ladies in the village of Champton St Mary, and partly because she believed that if you wed the passions of the moment, you will soon be widowed, and she did not want that.

'Miss March!' said Audrey, coming downstairs, pinny off, hair brushed, face on, in a wool suit in soft blue, her string of meagre pearls round her neck and a brooch that gave a little sparkle pinned to her breast. She looks like someone, thought Theo, and then realised it was the Queen, or the Queen if painted in watercolours. 'Merry Christmas – and you've brought something?'

'Yes,' said Miss March, 'just little things.' She handed Audrey an Elite Fashions bag filled with immaculately wrapped presents.

'Then they must go under the tree!' said Audrey, and immediately regretted it, because there was no present for Miss March.

Miss March, who missed little, did not miss this, and said quickly, 'And, please, Mrs Clement, I'm not expecting anything. Apart from the pleasure of being at your table today.'

'Come through, come through,' said Audrey, and shepherded her into their drawing room. Bernard was standing in front of the fire with his third glass of sherry.

'Miss March, you know Lord de Floures?'

'Yes, merry Christmas, m'lord,' said Miss March, and for an awful moment Audrey thought she might curtsey.

Bernard was not quite sure what to say for a moment, for his social antennae flashed contradictory messages – shopkeeper and fellow lunch guest – but he decided on 'Merry Christmas' because you can't go wrong with that, although he had once said it to the King of Jordan, descendant of the Prophet Muhammad, at an après-ski in Gstaad, but he hadn't seemed to mind. 'I hope we haven't ruined the day by imposing like this on your host?'

'I understand Mrs Shorely's sister has been taken ill. I hope it's nothing serious.'

'Mrs Shorely would not abandon us if it weren't. Heart attack. Or stroke. I don't know which is worse.'

'Stroke,' said Miss March. 'If it doesn't kill you, it can leave you very feeble.'

This had of course occurred to Bernard, and he was wondering if it were a stroke if Mrs Shorely might bring her invalid sister to live at Champton, for he did not see how he could do without her.

The thought sent a shadow across his mood. 'Yes, very . . . difficult . . .'

'Miss March,' said Audrey, 'anything chocolate in your presents?'

'No,' she said, 'nothing like that. Non-perishables only.'

'Poisonous to dogs, you see. I don't want to leave them under the tree and put temptation in their way.' 'Such lovely paper!'

'Oh, please don't bother,' said Miss March.

'But how thoughtful of you to want to contribute,' said Daniel – who had just returned from locking up after the service – in a parsonical way, 'just like the de Floures with the wine and the venison. Where *is* the venison?'

'Coming up the drive right now,' said Theo, looking out of the window.

Alex and Honoria were just arriving. Honoria had the large wicker basket she usually took shopping, picturesquely, in the King's Road covered with a cloth and Alex, in oven gloves, had an enormous stock pot, which he was carrying by the handles. Audrey went to meet them at the doorstep to direct them immediately into the kitchen. 'There's more in the Land Rover,' said Alex, so Theo, followed by the dogs, who were still shadowing him in the hope that they might get something tasty for their trouble, fetched a Christmas pudding from the back that Honoria had wrapped in foil and a dog blanket.

As Audrey took control of supplies in the kitchen, Theo went to see to the guests' refreshments in the drawing room: Shloer for Miss March, who did not drink, which made Bernard less inclined to make an effort; another sherry for him; a first sherry for Daniel. Then he made a pass round all three with the red-and-black checkerboard platter, which was now in a state of some disorder. Miss March had not had caviar before, although it was not caviar; she tried it and disliked it. Daniel, fussy, tried to tidy up the platter a bit as it came past him, but that irritated Theo, who said, 'Take one or don't take one . . .' so Daniel took one of each.

Alex and Honoria had been crisply ordered out of the kitchen after they had deposited their offerings and been given plates of hot appetisers – devils on horseback and prawn vol-au-vents – to take to the drawing room.

'Didn't you bring Jane and Victor?' said Bernard.

'They decided to walk, Daddy,' said Honoria.

'Jane? Walk?'

'I thought it odd too,' said Honoria, for her father's cousin was notorious for doing nothing energetic at all when she came to stay. Indeed, one Christmas, when she'd asked if she might watch the Furtho Hunt, which met at Champton on Boxing Day – not for bloodthirsty reasons but because she liked the scarlet and the hunting horns and the stirrup cup – she'd brought a special outfit for country sport and appeared wearing a pair of Chanel ballet flats and an Yves Saint Laurent yellow peplum blazer, which so startled a nervy hunter that the rider was nearly thrown. 'Scarlet is not the ONLY colour,' she'd said when Bernard had remonstrated with her, and that was the end of her enthusiasm for sport.

A gin and tonic was provided for Alex, and then Bernard wanted one too, and Honoria joined the Clements in a glass of fizz, which she thought would be champagne but was Henkell Trocken.

There was another ring on the doorbell. 'Ah, Jane and Victor!' said Bernard, but it was Neil Vanloo, who for Christmas Day had put on his court-appearance suit, in which he looked more like a defendant than a police officer, for he was built for sport, not elegance.

'Merry Christmas, one and all,' he said, and presented Theo with half a dozen bottles of Stella Artois and a bottle of Baileys. Next, to Miss March's relief, he presented Daniel with a bag of badly wrapped presents. 'Stick them under the tree, Dan. Don't get too excited.'

He crouched to greet the dogs, who came running over, for Neil was a reliable source of titbits and fuss. 'Who's a good boooy? Who's a good giiirl?' he said and both, like ships capsizing, slowly tipped onto their sides and then went belly-up so he could scratch their pinkish tummies. Daniel approached with the plate of devils on horseback and Neil took two, not for himself, but for the dogs, who immediately and obediently turned right side up again and sat. Never for me, thought Daniel, who had about as much control of the dogs as he did the weather. 'One for YOU,' said Neil, 'and one for YOU,' and the little delicacies were swallowed in a single snap, which seemed to Daniel to be rather a waste considering the amount of labour that went into their preparation. Audrey had decided to anoint the sausages with marmalade before putting them in the oven – an unlikely pairing that had created a sensation when they were served at the Braunstonbury Beagle Ball last January, and it did not go unnoticed today. Cosmo and Hilda were not gourmets and did not savour what they ate, but Bernard, Alex and Honoria were. Bernard resolved not to have a second one, Alex thought it a bit Delia, and Honoria could not remember the last time she had seen a cocktail sausage on a plate of canapés, let alone one sticky with marmalade.

Neil thought them a great success. 'It's like having your main and your sweet in one mouthful,' he said, and helped himself to two more. 'Miss March, have you tried one of these?'

Miss March smiled and shook her head and patted her stomach as if to say she was on a diet, but in truth she was chary of finger food, partly because a palette of pale greys increased the risk of grease spots on one's clothes, but mostly because she thought it vulgar. She had once read a book of etiquette written in Victorian England, which set out the rules for peeling and eating an orange with a fruit knife and fork, which pleased her so much she had practised at home and had looked, ever since, for an opportunity to perform this at another's table. Perhaps today?

There was another ring on the doorbell. Audrey had been waiting especially for this so almost ran out of the kitchen to open the door to Jane and Victor, who both had red spots on their cheeks and that slight tightness about the face that comes with exposure to cold. 'You must be *freezing*!' said Audrey as a great rush of steam from the kitchen fogged

Victor's glasses. When the dogs then rushed to greet them he was disconcerted because he did not like dogs much, and if there were to be dogs, he would prefer to be able to see where they were and what they were doing. He danced a dainty little ballet to keep his ankles out of range.

'Oh, you have dogs,' he said, a statement of plain fact, which nevertheless conveyed reproach.

'Cosmo! Hilda! Get DOWN!' said Audrey, confusing them because they were not actually up, just circling the new arrivals to check them out.

Jane, however, was more interested in talking about the cold weather than the dachshunds. '*So* cold, but we wrapped up *warmly*,' she said, and almost did a twirl.

Oh, thought Audrey, *now* I know why you chose to walk. 'Let me take your coat, Jane,' she said, pushing in front of Theo, for it was a fur. Not just fur; a sable, knee length, cut beautifully – she did not know you could tailor furs like that – with a Peter Pan collar and a waist and large flaps over the pockets. As she took it, she glanced at the label. It was white with red script – Oscar de la Renta. 'What a glorious thing,' she said.

'Thank you. Present from Santa,' said Jane. 'Lovely Santa, though if he had really thought it through, it would have been ankle length.' She gave her husband a sour little smile. 'My calves haven't been this cold since I was made to play lacrosse at St Leonard's.'

Audrey shepherded them into the drawing room. 'Dan, do the introductions, I'm in the kitchen.'

'Can I help?' said Honoria.

'Oh, yes, can . . . I?' said Jane as vaguely as possible.

'No, thank you!' said Audrey, who no more wanted help when she was cooking than a husband when she was giving birth. 'All under control!' and she went back to the kitchen, pausing only to run her hand down the luxurious garment hanging in the cloakroom. She resisted the temptation to bury her face in it.

'Mrs Cabot, Mr Cabot,' said Dan, 'this is Neil Vanloo . . .'

'Victor and Jane, Victor and Jane – please,' said Victor.

'. . . and this is Miss March.'

There was something about Miss March that made Victor hesitate to invite her to use their Christian names, so he just smiled and shook hands.

'Miss March, did I see you in church?' said Jane. 'I know we've met.'

'You called in at my shop yesterday, Mrs Cabot, just opposite the park gates.'

'Posh Frocks or something?'

'Elite Fashions.'

'Oh, yes . . .' She could not quite think of what to say or how to say it. 'The clothes . . . were lovely. And such a selection!'

'It's not Fifth Avenue,' said Miss March, 'but we're not New York.'

'Of course not.' She turned aside to take a glass of Henkell Trocken from Theo, then turned back. 'What are the well-dressed ladies of Champton wearing this season?'

'For formal, a high-street version of Margaret Thatcher. For everyday clothes, something that looks like what the Duchess of Devonshire wears on a quiet day at the Chatsworth Farm Shop. Jaeger always good. Country Casuals.'

'Two very stylish ladies,' said Jane, and she smiled her mean smile, which made Miss March think of someone biting unexpectedly on a caper.

Theo asked Victor if he would like a glass of fizz. 'No, thanks, Theo, I don't drink champagne . . .'

'Don't worry, it isn't that.'

'I don't want to risk a headache. Do you have any soda?'

'We have Shloer.'

'What is Shloer?'

Jane said, 'It's non-alcoholic grape juice. I've never actually tried it, but it should be fine.'

'Mum keeps some in for when the bishop comes – he doesn't drink either,' said Theo.

'A glass of that,' said Victor. 'And Mr ... Neil, wasn't it?'

'Yes, Neil Vanloo.'

'That doesn't sound like a British name.'

'It's not. Low Countries originally. And your surname?'

'Cabot.'

'Where's that from?'

Jane interrupted. 'Boston. Massachusetts, not Lincolnshire. But Jersey originally, the Channel Islands. Came over with the Founding Fathers.'

'Puritans?' asked Neil.

'Pirates,' said Jane.

'So we're all immigrants.'

'All Americans are immigrants.'

'Except the Indians.'

Jane gave him a look. 'I meant all Americans like us.'

'And you, Mr Van ...?' said Victor.

'Vanloo.'

'Whom did your people displace?'

'They didn't displace anyone. We're Moravian

Brethren. My family are. I'm not really anything now. But we started out in the Netherlands, I think, went to Germany, then finally came to England. To Oldham.'

'When was that?'

'In the 1780s. It was a missionary movement. In fact, the first Indian church in America was Moravian. Mohicans.'

'How colonial,' said Jane.

'They defended the Mohicans against the colonists. Didn't win them many friends.'

Victor tried to steer the conversation in a more amicable direction. 'And when was this?'

'The 1740s? I think it was near Poughkeepsie.'

'Where?' said Jane.

'Poughkeepsie?' Neil repeated. 'I don't know how you say it.'

'*Pa*kipsie,' she said. 'It's pronounced Pakipsie. What *are* these?'

Theo came by with a refreshed plate of devils on horseback. 'Devils on horseback.'

'Yes, I know, but there's some sort of sweet pickle on it.'

'It's marmalade.'

'Good lord!' said Jane.

'One of my mother's innovations,' said Daniel.

Theo offered them to Victor. 'No, thanks,' he said, 'I can't.'

'I thought that when I heard "marmalade" too,' said Theo, 'but it works.'

'It's not that. I have a strict diet.'

'Doctor's orders?'

'Nutritionist. I have allergies.'

Jane gave him a chilly look. 'No one's interested in that.'

Daniel said, 'But you must say if there's anything you can't eat. I'm sure we can find something you can.'

'Nonsense,' said Jane, 'he's fine with vegetables and . . . are we having turkey?'

'There's turkey and venison.'

'Ours?' asked Jane.

'It's from the estate. Does that make a difference?'

It made no nutritional difference at all, but Jane would not let an opportunity to remind her interlocutors of the social distance pass.

'Turkey is fine. Or perhaps there are . . . innovations? Shall I ask your mother?'

'Good luck with that,' said Theo.

In the kitchen there was one more salmon and caviar checkerboard and one more plate of devils on horseback waiting on the kitchen table. Audrey, in her pinny, had a look of intense concentration and stood in front of the Aga looking like a virtuoso playing a xylophone. She was moving pans of vegetables so they sat half on the hot plate, opening the warming oven with her foot, and at the same time keeping a fixed eye on the bread sauce, which had been cooking very slowly in the bain-marie on a simmering plate. How she loved this sort of thing, Daniel thought, not only cooking a full-complement Christmas lunch but for a guestlist doubled with a day's notice.

'How far off are we, Mum?'

She paused for a moment to make a mental calculation. 'Eleven minutes to serving. Give them another round of nibbles, then get them to the table. What did you think of *Cousin Jane's* coat?' She said 'Cousin Jane' with a slight emphasis for sarcasm.

'I didn't really notice.'

'Yes, you did.'

'A fur.'

'A *fur*? Oscar de la Renta. I looked at the label. Sable. Must have cost a bomb. And did you notice she complained about it? Not long enough! What does he do? Victor?'

'I don't know. Family money? Wall Street?'

'There's something not right about him.'

'What do you mean?'

'A fake. He's trying to look like a country gent. Oh, God, is the hostess trolley on?'

The little orange light glowed. 'Yes. Do you want me to do anything? Do you want Honoria?'

'Take those nibbles through, and then get them to the table in . . . ten minutes.'

Theo was refilling Honoria and Alex's glasses.

'What is this fizz?' said Alex.

'Henkell Trocken,' said Theo. 'A Sekt. We always have it at Christmas.'

'German wine. Very underrated,' he said.

'It's not Bollinger,' said Theo, 'but . . . I don't know, we just always have it. Cheaper than Bolly, that's for sure.'

Daniel appeared with the plates of nibbles.

'That chessboard looks very pretty,' said Honoria, 'I don't want to spoil the effect . . .'

Alex dived in and took two of the salmon, so she felt honour bound to take two of the caviar, which wasn't caviar. She started to eat one, and decided one was more than enough.

'Are you sure I can't help in the kitchen?' she said. 'At least with the venison?'

'Come not between the dragon and her Aga,' said Theo.

'Dragon?'

'Mum doesn't like having people around her when she's cooking,' said Daniel.

Honoria was not quite prepared to give up. 'There's redcurrant jelly – Mrs Shorely made it – in the basket, and brandy butter for the pudding, and I forgot to tell Audrey but I put in a whole Stilton from Paxton & Whitfield. And a ham.'

'So generous of you, thank you. But a firm no to the offer of help.' That, Daniel thought, would knock the modest chunk of Stilton Audrey had got from Sainsbury's off the cheeseboard, and then he had a feeling of anxiety that they didn't have a scoop, for he felt sure the de Floures would scoop, not cut, a Stilton, and the Clements cut – not that it mattered, only it did matter a bit, he realised, or he wouldn't have noticed. It would matter to Audrey, which is where he got it from, who would feel marked down if there were a moment of scoop/slice anxiety.

He moved on to Bernard, who was talking dutifully to Miss March.

'And how do you know what the ladies are going to like when you order the fashions for next year?'

'Knowing your customers is essential for retailers.'

'I don't suppose the ladies of Champton and the Badsaddles are suddenly going to surprise one by turning up to the Flower Festival in . . . space suits.'

'Probably not, nor do they need front-row seats at New York Fashion Week' – Alex, who was standing nearby, looked up at this – 'to anticipate what Mrs Porteous and Mrs Staveley and Mrs Braines will be wearing for Easter. Usually there's a certain shade, an accessory, that captures their imagination.'

Alex joined them. 'Are you a regular at New York Fashion Week, Miss March?'

'I am not.'

'But did you notice what Cousin Jane was wearing?'

'I think I caught a glimpse through the door.'

'How magnificent of Father Christmas, don't you think?' said Alex.

'It would be difficult to imagine anything more magnificent.'

'Too much?' he asked.

'I couldn't say.'

'I thought it looked like something Elizabeth Taylor would wear to Camp David.'

Miss March took a sip of Shloer. 'Perhaps not an unimaginable scenario in Mrs Cabot's world.'

'I only wear two things,' said Bernard, 'tweeds for

country, dark suit for town, and I never go to town, so only one thing.'

'You sometimes go mad and sport cavalry twill trousers, Daddy,' said Alex.

'So I do. Am I supposed to think about my trousers?'

'And you have a morning suit for weddings.'

'My father's. I am fortunate, Miss March, to be the same shape as my papa.'

'And you have that bowler hat and umbrella outfit for regimental things.'

'It is not an *outfit*, Alex,' said Bernard, peeved, 'it's the correct dress for parade in town, it's *uniform*. And I don't really go to those any more, or not if I can help it.'

'And he dodged the Lord Lieutenancy because he didn't want to wear the kit. Or buy the kit.'

Bernard, stung by this, said, 'Have a care, Alex.'

Miss March quickly said, 'I think it's marvellous that you are wearing your father's clothes. And what a testament to his tailor that they are still wearable.'

'I never really think about it,' growled Bernard. 'I don't have to. If you were less of a peacock, Alex, you might turn your mind to more profitable matters than – what's the line from the hymn? – boasted pomp and show.'

You don't think about it because you don't have to, thought Miss March, because you have nothing to prove to the world when prestige is your birthright; but she said, 'Solid joys and lasting treasures none but Zion's children know,' and Bernard nodded.

Audrey then appeared in the doorway, pinny off, but still slightly pink from the kitchen. '*À table*,' she said, '*à table!*'

Audrey, who normally dropped off to sleep in an instant, had lain awake for an hour the night before, fretting about the *placement*, as she called it. She and Daniel sat at opposite ends of the dining table in the rectory's lovely dining room, the mirror image of the drawing room, only with a large window overlooking the walled garden behind the house. It was panelled – 'Queen Anne baroque', according to Daniel – and hung with paintings that came with the house, of former incumbents; a parsons' ancestry, not of birth but vocation. Actually, some of the former incumbents had been de Floures, fruits of an overstocked nursery, given the living when something to occupy them had to be found, so the walls showed almost a clash of claims on the past, patrons versus incumbents, with the doubly qualified in the wigs and bands of their profession and the coppery hair and blue eyes of their genes.

How that worked out in the *placement* was complicated. Daniel at the head and she at the foot was straightforward, but who would sit at Daniel's right hand and who at hers? Bernard, surely, took precedence, so on her right he would go. The conversation would not be the breeziest, but at least they were known quantities to each other. The place to Daniel's right would then, by convention, go to Lady de Floures, but as the last to occupy the post had left Bernard and returned to Siena, did that mean 'Cousin Jane' was next in line? But Daniel would want Miss March there, she supposed, for she was furthest from honour, and what with the first being last and all that. And if she *did* go there, where would Victor go? She could bunch the young 'uns, as she thought of them – Theo and Honoria and Alex – in the middle, but what about Neil Vanloo? Should she put him and Miss March together, a sort of blue-collar corner, or would that look like social purdah? How rude! But she could not imagine the conversation flowing between Neil Vanloo and Jane Cabot, so perhaps it would be better . . . She dreamt that night of the signing of the Treaty of Versailles and everyone falling out at the last minute because she had messed up the protocol, and howitzer shells exploded and shattered the Hall of Mirrors into smithereens.

Daniel in the end had acquiesced and so Jane Cabot was seated on his right, Bernard on Audrey's right. Clockwise from Daniel it went Miss March, Victor, Theo, Bernard, Audrey, Honoria, Neil, Alex and Jane, but Alex looked in before lunch and switched Theo and Honoria, partly because he wanted Honoria to be next to Bernard to keep him under control and partly because he wanted to separate Honoria and Neil, because they had a secret history – not so secret, actually, but a certain distance might help sustain the necessary goodwill of the season.

All were in their reappointed places save Audrey, who made a brilliant entrance pushing the creaking hostess trolley in from the kitchen. It was so heavily laden it began to lean to the right and for a moment it looked like it might tip the turkey and the venison onto the floor. Neil intervened with a corrective manoeuvre and there were two rounds of applause, the first for his rescue, then a second for the magnificence of the roasted meats on their dishes, the golden high-breasted turkey, the blood-red haunch of venison. (Is that what a haunch looks like? thought Miss March.)

Audrey parked the trolley next to the sideboard. 'Shall I carve?' she said, a question that needed no answer because she took up the carving knife and the steel and started sharpening it with a sort of focused fury that made Daniel think of that bit of the Prophecy of Ezekiel about a sword being sharpened to make a sore slaughter.

'Let me help,' he said, and transferred the dishes to the sideboard, then opened the top of the hostess trolley to reveal a row of lidded Pyrex dishes in which carrots and French beans and sprouts were slowly losing structure in the mini Turkish bath this inelegant way of serving boiled vegetables provided.

Theo got up too and took a claret jug from the opposite sideboard, which he had filled earlier, the angel's measure lost not to evaporation but his own thirst.

'Ah, is that my claret?' said Bernard in a faintly seigneurial way. 'Looks more handsome than it deserves in that jug, ha-ha!' He laughed at his own witticism in the way of someone who needs to fill an anticipated silence.

'It is, and thank you,' said Theo, starting to pour for Jane, whom he instinctively knew to be the one to whom that honour should go.

'Not for Victor,' she said, 'sulphides.'

'Oh, come on, it's the holidays!' Victor said.

'You can if you want to, but you know you'll pay for it if you do.'

'Just a small glass?'

'On your own head be it.'

Theo poured a full measure of wine into Victor's glass. He noticed Jane's lips purse as she said, 'Do you have any water?'

'Normal water. I don't think we've got mineral.'

'Tap is fine.' Jane got up. 'Point me to the kitchen, and where can I find a jug and a glass? A tumbler?'

Theo said in an exaggerated American accent, 'A pitcher of iced water?'

'Exactly that,' said Victor, 'and thank you.'

'Give me a minute,' said Theo.

'Allow me,' said Jane. 'You're busy. Where are the glasses?'

Theo said, 'In the corner cupboard over there. There should be a jug there too, for Pimm's.'

'You have ice?'

'Top of the fridge. In the utility room, next to the kitchen.'

Audrey was at that moment testing the turkey to see that it was properly cooked through, an assessment which required a certain delicacy in front of those who were about to eat it, and Daniel was fetching the plates from the trolley's warming shelf and arranging them fussily in a line along the sideboard. Audrey looked up from the steaming fowl and said in her brightly menacing tone, 'Theo will take care of that, Jane!'

Jane was already taking a glass and a jug from the cupboard. 'I don't want our colonial habits to cause you any trouble, Audrey . . .'

'Really, dear, it is no trouble . . .'

Now Jane was heading for the door to the kitchen. 'I'll just follow my nose,' she said, 'and it smells *so* delicious.'

Audrey gave Theo a meaningful look, but he was too busy thinking about the wine to notice.

Honoria noticed. 'Jane, let me?' she said, getting up, but Jane was gone. 'Can I hand things round, Audrey?' she said.

Audrey made a snap decision. 'Dan, carve and do the roast potatoes. There are parsnips too – don't get them mixed up; Honoria, you do the vegetables; I'll go and fetch the gravy and the . . . extras.'

Audrey handed over the carving knife and fork to Daniel. 'Different knife for the venison, I think – use Granny's with the ivory handle that's loose, and be careful. You will have to make do with the one fork,' and she handed him the cutlery like a squire arming his knight.

She patted down her pinny and scooted off towards the kitchen.

There she found Jane, not by the sink where the tap was unturned and the jug remained unfilled, but standing over the Aga, leaning over it in fact, as if the savoury vapours rising from the bain-marie and the gravy pan might thus be analysed better.

'Jane, you wanted a jug of water?'

Jane turned. 'Oh, yes, I couldn't find . . .'

'The tap is over the sink, dear, where it usually is.' She smiled. 'The cold one is marked with a C.'

'Yes,' said Jane, pretending not to notice the barb, 'but I'm so *intrigued* by these . . .' – she extended her hands over the hot plates – 'extras?'

'Just some gravy and bits and bobs . . .'

'So much *work* . . .'

'Not really . . .'

'And I haven't had bread sauce since . . . I think it was after a shoot here, years ago.' She fanned her hand over the slowly bubbling bain-marie and sniffed. 'What is it . . . nutmeg?'

'Not nutmeg, no . . .'

'Cloves, definitely . . .'

'Just store-cupboard basics . . .'

'Oh, and the *richness*, the butter . . . and cream?'

'Top of the milk, if you have any, but let me . . .'

'And there's bay and there's . . . something else.'

'Oh, it will stick and burn!' said Audrey, and half shoved Jane out of the way to rescue the sauce, which didn't need rescuing, for that was the whole point of the bain-marie.

'What is it? The something else? Clotted cream?' She sniffed again. 'Cinnamon?'

Audrey said nothing but stirred the bread sauce with a purpose that suggested that as far as she was concerned the conversation was over. Jane said, 'The gravy's lovely and . . . rich,' and gave a little shrug.

'*Do* help yourself to water, Jane,' said Audrey. 'There's a lemon in the pantry. Next to the utility. Ice in the freezer. Through there. *There.*' She pointed with her wooden spoon and a blob of bread sauce detached and plopped onto the tiled floor where it settled more than spread, like a Welsh cake dropped on a griddle. Ooh, thought Audrey, that's *à point*.

All were seated round the table. A jug of iced water stood in front of Victor; wine glowed in their glasses, lit by flickers from the candles and the fire; Miss March looked at the cracker over her dessert spoon and fork and wondered if she would be expected to suffer the indignity of a paper crown. Plates loaded with turkey or venison (for Theo both) and roast potatoes, with parsnips and Brussels sprouts and pigs in blankets, and stuffing for those who had chosen turkey and a chestnut purée that Honoria had brought in a tub from London for those who had chosen venison, were in front of those bidden to share the great feast.

Audrey was enjoying a moment of triumph. Around her table her guests awaited: a peer of the realm! Two Honourables (perhaps three; she wasn't sure if Jane was one or not)! A Boston Brahmin! Her marvellous sons! Her eye rather glided over Miss March and Detective Sergeant Vanloo, and instead took in the magnificence of her table. Silver glowed and crystal shone; the plates were laden with food; she had bought paper napkins in what she thought was a Christmas tartan; holly and ivy had been carefully strewn around the candlesticks and the placemats between them, on which stood two gravy boats, a dish of cranberry sauce, a dish of redcurrant jelly and, in the middle, a lidded bowl of bread sauce in a quantity that would surely exceed the accumulated appetites of all her guests.

She sat, which Bernard took as a cue to start, but as he reached for the gravy Daniel stood and said,

'Let us pray . . .' which made him freeze so his sleeve hovered over his plate. 'For these and all his gifts,' said Daniel, 'may God's name be thanked and praised . . .'

'Amen!' said Bernard, but Daniel wasn't done.

'. . . and as we celebrate this great feast, let us be mindful of the needs of those who will go hungry today, the homeless, the lonely, all who suffer depriv- ation as a consequence of conflict and injustice . . .'

Bernard couldn't keep his arm extended for a litany of the unfortunate, so he slowly retracted it in a way that he hoped would be unnoticeable, but he accidentally dragged his sleeve through the pile of chestnut purée on his plate, which clung to the tweed so tenaciously that there was more lost in transit than left in situ. Theo was rather transfixed by this and when Daniel concluded – '. . . we ask this, through Our Incarnate Lord, Jesus Christ, in whose name all gifts are blessed . . .' – he missed the 'Amen' and then crossed himself jerkily, which startled Bernard, whose hand jerked too in an involuntary response, and there followed one of those distinctively Church of England moments of confusion when no one was sure what they were meant to do, and a little Mexican wave of uncertain movement passed round the table.

Daniel sat down.

'Oh, how ... gymnastic,' said Jane, reaching reso-
lutely for the bread sauce.

It was the Clements' custom to pull crackers between the turkey and the Christmas pudding, so
after helping Audrey and Honoria to clear away,
Miss March had found herself in the unwelcome
situation of having to cross her arms to oblige Victor
on her left, and Daniel on her right. Victor was no
expert in cracker pulling and pulled too hard, which
wrenched Miss March's arm and sent the contents
of her cracker spinning through the air like shrap-
nel. Theo retrieved them, including a little plastic
referee's whistle, which she blew very faintly once
to look like she was getting into the spirit of things.

They all read out the terrible jokes on the slips of
paper inside.

'Who commits espionage in the kitchen at
Christmas?' asked Victor.

Your wife, thought Audrey, but she said nothing.

'Mince spies!' he said. 'I don't get it, but I know
it's funny!'

Bernard didn't understand his and made a mess
of it, and in the faintly awkward silence that followed Audrey put on her paper crown and everyone
followed suit. Miss March, who was fastidious to

an extraordinary degree in matters of dress, hated this custom but felt obliged, and then dismayed, for when she unpeeled hers she discovered it to be a most unflattering shade of orange.

Honoria emptied Victor's cracker of the rest of its bounty and he put on the purple crown so enthusiastically it tore. Then something fluttered to the floor.

'What's that?' asked Victor.

'It's your gift,' said Honoria, 'and look, it's my favourite, the Fortune Teller Miracle Fish!'

'What does it do?'

Honoria took a little fish-shaped piece of dark-red cellophane out of the printed envelope and held it by the tail. She said, 'You put it on your hand – hold your hand out, Victor, like so – and then, depending on how the fish curls, your future will be revealed.'

'What kind of future?'

'You'll meet a tall, dark stranger, or silver will cross your palm, or beware the Ides of March – I don't know, it all depends on whether it curls up from the nose or the tail or the sides. There's a code on the back of the envelope. Yes, if only the head moves it means you're jealous. The tail means indifferent. If both move, you're in love, and if it turns completely over, you're false. Want to see?'

'Sure!' he said.

She placed the Fortune Teller Fish on the palm of his hand, which immediately curled up so violently it did a sort of somersault.

'False!' said Honoria. 'The fish has spoken!'

'What was that?' said Jane from the other side of the table. 'Who is false?'

'You should know, you married him,' said Honoria, but then regretted it because Jane did not seem to find that amusing. 'It's just a silly cracker novelty, Jane. Why don't you have a go?'

'But what is it?'

'It's a fish that tells your fortune when you place it on your hand,' said Daniel.

'Isn't that against the rules for vicars?'

'I don't think I quite take it that seriously, Jane. I think there's just some sort of coating that reacts with the sweat on your hand.'

'Oh, how lovely,' said Jane. 'I think I'll pass.'

Audrey saw an opportunity. 'Have a go, Jane, it's just a silly game! And we have a tradition never to ignore the teaching of the Fortune Teller Fish.'

'Do we?' said Theo.

'We do,' said Audrey. 'Pass the thing over, Victor.'

Victor obliged, in that moment keener to appease his hostess than his wife. Alex took it by the tail and waved it in front of Jane's face. 'Hold out your hand, Cousin Jane. Or are you afeared of the Fortune Teller Fish?'

'Don't be ridiculous, Alex,' said Jane and held out her hand.

Alex laid it on her palm. Nothing happened. It did not so much as stir, let alone curl up or somersault.

'Great,' said Jane, 'non-sweaty hands, I'll take that. It means hygienic,' and she flashed a little smile at Audrey.

'It means death,' said Neil. 'Technically it means you're dead, if it does nothing.'

'Well, I refute the prophecy thus,' said Jane, silencing the Fortune Teller Fish by scrunching it up in her fist.

There was silence for a moment.

Audrey said, 'Pudding?'

Chapter Five

The Christmas pudding had burnt with a satis-
factory blue flame, only slightly scorching the sprig
of holly stuck in it. It was almost impossibly rich
– 'I find the brandy butter rather cuts that richness,'
said Bernard, heaping it like mashed potato onto his
plate. Jane asked for a fruit plate as a substitute for
Victor and he got the fruit bowl. The silver sixpence
buried within the pudding, preserved for this use
in the Clement family for three generations, went
to Honoria, who declared her find. Jane said, 'See,
it's not only the nuts that could have choked you,
Victor.'

Theo had found a bottle of Tokay at the back
of the drinks cabinet, which Audrey thought might
have been acquired by one of her great-aunts,
but the contents were delicious and added to the
somnolence that began to fall over the table in

anticipation of the fading winter light outside. The Stilton, magnificent and proud on its cheese board, a serving spoon doubling as a scoop laid casually to one side, was untouched, like the dates and the glacé fruits and the mandarin oranges. The nutcracker lay unused in the bowl of Brazils and hazelnuts and almonds and walnuts.

The fire suddenly spat and roused Audrey, who looked at the clock on the mantelpiece and shouted 'The Queen!' so loudly she roused everyone else. She shooed all her guests into the drawing room, and as three o'clock struck from the church tower the television screen lit up to reveal royal trumpeters in scarlet and gold playing a fanfare as the Queen came onstage at a Save the Children concert at the Royal Albert Hall wearing a dress that made even the fervently loyal Miss March think 'shower curtain'. Surrounded by children of many nations, rather than the familiar backdrop of Windsor Castle or Buckingham Palace, she invited the young of the Commonwealth to consider environmental issues and then went backstage, looking more uncomfortable among her guileless questioners, Daniel thought, than in a press of world leaders.

There was another awkward moment when the National Anthem was played and Bernard thought it proper to stand, so everybody else had to also, but he rather struggled to get out of the sofa he had been directed to sit on, and by the time he was up the sovereign was already victorious, happy and glorious, and everyone else was looking to sit down.

Miss March was the next to be discomfited because Alex said, 'Did I see presents under the tree?'

Audrey said, 'Yes, you did, but—'

Daniel interrupted. 'I don't think we—'

'Anything for me?' said Alex.

'I don't think there are presents for *everyone*,' said Daniel. 'Some have given gifts in other ways, so it might look a bit *uneven* . . .'

'You can't just leave them there,' said Alex. 'Let's go and see who's been a good little boy or girl and who hasn't.'

He flung open the door to the hall and made them all troop out and form an awkward semicircle around the tree.

Before anyone could intervene Alex, like a nine-year-old, was on his knees and sorting through the shallow pile that lay there. 'One for me, two for me; one wrapped rather well, the other . . .' He opened the well-wrapped one from Miss March first, tearing the end rather than undoing the ribbon and the impeccably Sellotaped joins, which made her wince. Inside, wrapped in tissue paper, was a tartan lambswool scarf. 'Oh,' he said, 'that *does* look comfy, and so Scotch. Thank you, Miss March,' and then he put it aside and opened the badly wrapped one from Neil, which barely needed opening, and it was a wind-up, brightly painted tin duck sitting on a tricycle with a rotor on his head that went round when he pedalled.

'I hope you like it,' said Neil. 'I got it at the market.'

'I LOVE it, so *Christmassy*!' said Alex, and got it going so it careered round the hall chased by Cosmo and Hilda, who barked loudly in misguided triumph when it wound down and gently toppled over.

Bernard got a scarf too in the same tartan as Alex. It had been carefully chosen – Ancient Campbell – not for colour and design, but because Miss March had looked up the de Floures family tree and found a daughter of a duke of Argyll in their recent lineage. Bernard seemed not to know, or particularly care, but held it up to admire it, said thank you, dropped the wrapping paper on the floor and later the scarf on the bench by the front door.

There were woollen gloves in a version of Fair Isle for Audrey and Honoria and Jane – fine for the former two, but Miss March winced again to think of them emerging from the sable sleeves of an Oscar de la Renta coat.

'They're gorgeous, thank you so much,' said Jane, admiring them without putting them on.

Miss March's embarrassment was mitigated by the next round of presents from Neil. Fish and chips had been wrapped more neatly, and the paper, tissue-thin and printed with robins and holly, fell away to reveal not gold, frankincense and myrrh, for these were not available at Braunstonbury Market on Christmas Eve, but a tin of Quality Street for Audrey, Groucho Marx specs with nose and moustache and eyebrows attached for Theo, mint Matchmakers for Miss March, one of those biros that could write in different colours for Daniel, and a tiny bottle of eau de parfum from Tramp for Honoria, which made Alex laugh.

'That's all I've got,' said Neil. 'Sorry, if I missed you out.'

'That's *quite* all right,' said Jane.

Theo put on his Groucho Marx specs. 'Do you wanna play charades?' he said to Miss March, rhyming it with parades, and waggling an imaginary cigar.

Miss March would no sooner have performed the dance of the Sugar Plum Fairy but she said nothing.

Theo moved on to Victor. 'Do *you* wanna play charades?'

'Sure,' said Victor, 'I love charades!'

'Just a minute,' said Jane.

'No charades?' said Victor with a note of impatience.

'Yes, charades, but there's another custom of the season you seem to be forgetting.' She pointed up.

The pale greeny-grey ball of mistletoe was directly overhead.

Victor looked surprised. 'You mean you want . . .?'

'What does everybody do under the mistletoe?' said Jane. Daniel noticed Neil and Honoria both take a little step back towards the wall.

'Merry Christmas, darling,' said Jane, and she went to embrace her husband. She more than embraced him; she planted her mouth on his in a way that went beyond the far edge of convivial. Miss March winced yet again.

'Jane,' said Honoria, 'you *are* full of good cheer.'

'Anyone else?' said Jane.

They all took a step back.

Miss March made the error of being the first to get Theo's charade.

'Book and film, three words. First word,' he mimed, and put his fingers together to form a T.

'The . . .' said Daniel.

Theo thought for a second or two. Then he made a big circle shape – 'Whole thing,' said Alex – and did a little comic run from one end of the drawing room to the other and back again.

'*The Loneliness of the Long Distance Runner*?' shouted Neil.

Theo shook his head and held up three fingers again.

'Three words,' said Audrey.

He ran again from one wall to the other and back again and looked around the circle of non-plussed faces, trying to chivvy them into making a guess.

'*Chariots of Fire*?' said Bernard.

'Begins with "The", Daddy,' said Honoria.

Theo thought again for a moment. Then mimed writing something and putting it into an envelope, and then he ran again from one wall to the other and back again.

'*Postman Pat*!' said Audrey. 'With his black and white cat!'

Theo said, 'Oh, Mum, film and a book, begins with "The"?'

'You're not allowed to speak!' shouted Alex. '*Nul points!*'

'*The Go-Between!*' blurted out Miss March.

'Yes!' said Theo. '*Thank you*, Miss March!'

The triumph of having got it right turned to ashes in an instant as she realised it was now her go. 'I'll pass my go to someone else,' she said. 'I'm a far better guesser than a doer.' This was met with dissent from everyone but Daniel, for no one knows better than a parson what agonies the shy have to endure.

'Nonsense,' said Alex, 'rules are rules.'

'*You* can have it,' Miss March replied, calculating correctly that he would not be able to resist a chance to take the stage. Alex was for a second divided, wanting a turn for himself but also wanting to discomfit Miss March, for he felt shyness was a moral failing that should not be indulged. In a moment of inspiration, he saw he could have both.

He stood in front of the fire and indicated a book – 'I don't know if it's a film or a television programme too; it probably is' – one word, three syllables.

He motioned to Miss March to stand and practically pulled her out of the chair when she shook her head. He got her to face the others and made the sign for 'the whole thing'. Then he poked her in the tummy.

It was not hard, but it was not welcome, or warranted, and Miss March, who particularly disliked being touched, recoiled.

No one said anything, so he did it again.

'Belly!' said Victor.

Alex shook his head.

Audrey shouted, 'Tummy trouble?'

'A poke?' said Neil.

'*Rosemary's Baby*?' said Theo.

Alex shook his head again. Then he poked her again.

'Enough,' said Daniel, 'we're not going to get it.'

'You haven't tried!'

'Enough, Alex,' said Daniel in a tone rarely heard. Everyone was silent. Then Alex shrugged.

Audrey, who never seemed to notice mood changes, or perhaps care about them, said, 'But what was it, Alex?'

'*Middlemarch.*'

'Brilliant!' said Audrey. 'But nobody got it, so who's turn is it now?'

'I go again.'

'You nominate someone,' said Daniel quickly. 'House rules.'

'Then I nominate Victor,' said Alex.

'I've got one,' said Victor and went to stand in front of them. 'What's the sign for a movie?'

'No talking!' said Alex snippily. 'There are *rules*.'

They all mimed a film camera being cranked.

'OK! Sorry!' said Victor.

He cranked.

'Film!' they said.

He held up three fingers.

'Three words!'

He held up one finger.

'First word!'

He mimed a pistol and shot Jane, which struck Audrey as unhusbandly, but she said nothing.

'Shoot!'

'Gun!'

'Murder?'

'*Murder on the Orient Express*?'

He shook his head.

'Pistol?'

'Bullet?'

He shook his head again and held up two fingers.

'Second word.'

He thought for a moment and then loosened his collar.

'Collar!'

'Hot?'

He shook his head, then pretended to write something. Then he looked up in a fey way, as if for inspiration, and wrote again.

'Oscar Wilde!'

He mimed a 'sort of'.

'Shakespeare?'

Another 'sort of'.

'*Hamlet!*'

He shook his head, tried to loosen his collar again and gulped.

'Strangle?'

'Throttle?'

He shook his head.

'Do the whole thing?' said Honoria.

He made a circle.

'The whole thing!'

He mimed writing again, then looked up for inspiration, took a couple of mincing steps, then fell to the floor dramatically, clutching at his throat.

'Molière!' said Theo.

'Why Molière?'

'Playwright! Collapsed on stage in the middle of a show and died!'

'But it's a film, three words . . .'

Victor shuddered and lay still.

'Got it,' said Honoria. '*Dead Poets Society*!'

'Brilliant!' said Alex and they all applauded. 'And marvellous performance, Victor, you should get the Oscar.'

But Victor did not stir.

Then Neil leapt out of his seat.

Chapter Six

'. . . twelve, thirteen, fourteen, fifteen . . .' Neil stopped compressions, tilted Victor's head back, put his mouth again over his, pinched his nose and breathed.

'His chest is moving,' said Theo, but it was because Neil was inflating his lungs.

He checked again for a pulse.

'Let me take over for a minute,' said Audrey, and without waiting for an answer she started compressions again. 'One, two, three, four . . .'

Daniel thought he heard a rib crack. 'Mum, go easy!'

Audrey, who had been resuscitating the lifeless since she had been a nurse in the Blitz, ignored him: '. . . nine, ten, eleven, twelve . . .'

Daniel said, 'Alex, see where that ambulance has got to.'

'There's a strike, remember, and it's Christmas Day. You couldn't pick a worse day to have a heart attack.'

Daniel winced, and instinctively looked to see if Jane had heard, but Jane wasn't in the drawing room. Bernard had taken her out to the kitchen, for he thought it no seemlier for a wife to witness a husband's death than a father the birth of a child. Miss March and Honoria had gone with them to make tea and be reassuring and to see that Jane did not help herself to another stiffening tot.

Neil, with help from Audrey, kept the effort up for half an hour before the ambulance arrived, blue lights flashing. Honoria, watching from the kitchen, thought twinkling blue was not really a Christmassy colour at all.

The ambulance crew knew Neil from his professional life and spoke to him as professionals do, without the softening gloss applied to white-faced relatives surrounding a body. For Victor was now a body, his life extinct almost as soon as he fell.

There were no flashing blue lights on the police car that was next to arrive. Another quiet conference took place between Neil and the officers and the ambulance crew, while Audrey made a pot of tea using one of the big teapots with two handles that no parsonage is without. She then made another, to provide refreshment for the emergency services, and quietly cast an eye around the kitchen to see if any secrets of her cuisine could be deduced from what had not yet been replaced in the pantry. There was something about Jane that suggested, even with the pressing matter of her husband's sudden death, that an opportunity to solve a mystery might be hard to resist. Honoria had started to wash up, making herself useful at this most testing time, but when Neil came in he stopped her.

'Please don't wash anything up, Honoria.'

'I am capable of housework, you know?' she said, stung.

'Evidence,' he replied. She took off her Marigolds and sat down.

'Evidence?' said Daniel.

'I am sorry to have to tell you—'

'I know,' said Jane, 'he's dead. We all know.'

'I am sorry for your loss,' said Neil, using the solemn *pro forma* the occasion required.

'Jane, how awful, I'm so sorry,' said Audrey.

'I could use a drink, Honoria,' said Jane. 'Scotch if there is any.'

'There is,' said Theo, and he went to fetch it. He stopped at the door. 'Anyone else?'

Nods came in response.

'I'll bring the bottle.'

Alex said, 'What do you mean, *evidence*?'

'Victo— Mr Cabot's diet was . . . particular.'

'He had to be careful with dairy,' said Jane, 'with glutens, with wine – the sulphides – and cigarette smoke, and caffeine. Cheese gave him a migraine – histamines apparently – so did smoked fish. And there was eczema and urticaria and, of course, nuts.'

'Nuts?'

'Made him very ill. Some nuts. Almonds, walnuts, hazelnuts . . . hazelnuts, were there hazelnuts in anything, Audrey?'

'No, only in the nut bowl, but he wouldn't have accidentally eaten a hazelnut.'

'Could something he was allergic to have caused him to get into physical distress?' said Neil.

'Not the cheese or wine, but the nuts. Yes, when he was younger, he used to have a fit of some kind, but not so bad now. You think it was a reaction to something?'

'How careful were you?'

'Very careful.'

'Marzipan!' said Audrey. 'There's marzipan in the Christmas cake! Almonds!'

'We haven't cut it yet, Mum,' said Daniel. 'It's in the pantry.'

'Oh, thank God,' said Audrey.

Theo returned with the bottle of the Macallan, which made Audrey wince, for there was a perfectly good bottle of Teacher's that she thought a better choice for a medicinal tot than a twelve-year-old Speyside single malt.

'Anything else you can think of?' asked Neil.

'Me?' said Audrey.

'Anything else that could have nuts in it? The stuffing?'

'He didn't have stuffing. All he got was a slice of turkey breast, a few sprouts and a dollop of gravy.'

'You're sure?'

'Yes. Jane supervised every morsel.'

'There is one thing . . .' said Jane.

'What one thing?'

'Your divine bread sauce, Audrey.'

Theo gasped, then pretended to cough.

'What about my bread sauce?'

'What's in it?' asked Jane.

Audrey tried to speak, but nothing came at first.

She opened her mouth again, then closed it. Then she said, 'Bread.'

'Bread and . . .?'

'Bread and milk and butter. And an onion. And some bits and bobs.'

'What bits and bobs?' Jane asked.

If it had been a lawcourt rather than her kitchen, Audrey would have asked to approach the bench. 'No nuts . . .' But there was something she was not saying.

'I need to know everything, Audrey, *everything*,' said Jane.

How wicked of Jane, thought Audrey, to use her husband's unexplained death as a pretext to wrench her most treasured recipe out of her hands. 'Bay leaf. Cloves. You stud the onion with cloves. For the milk infusion.'

'Is that all?'

Audrey suddenly felt like a Rhinemaiden swimming around the Nibelung horde at the bottom of the river.

'More or less.'

'What else, Audrey?' asked Neil, sounding ominously official.

There was silence. Then she said, in the breezy tone she always used in defeat, 'There was a sprinkle – no more – of mace.'

'Of *course*,' said Jane, 'that's what I couldn't place.'

'Mace?' said Neil.

'It's a spice,' said Audrey. 'You might have had it with . . .' – she struggled to think what Neil growing up in Lancashire might have had it with – 'potted shrimps?'

'It's made from the outer casing of a nutmeg,' said Daniel, then he added, 'which interestingly is the only single tree to produce two different spices.'

'So, a nut?' said Neil.

'Nutmeg's not a nut,' said Audrey, 'it's a seed. Like tomato is not a vegetable, but a fruit.'

'But it's still an allergen,' said Jane. 'I once nearly lost Victor to an eggnog. It was the nutmeg!'

'But mace is *not* nutmeg,' said Audrey. 'I *told* you there was no nutmeg in my bread sauce.'

'It's got the same damn chemicals in it,' said Jane.

'Barely a pinch. And as I said' – she looked to Daniel for support – 'it's not a nut, so how could it pose a risk?'

'Why didn't you *say*?' said Jane.

'I don't give a comprehensive list of ingredients for everything I serve, dear,' said Audrey, but then she remembered that Jane's husband had just died on her drawing-room floor and checked her sarcasm.

'You said you would make sure there was nothing on Victor's plate that could harm him.'

'But how was I to know the bread sauce – your famous bread sauce that everyone goes on about – was laced with allergens?'

'Really, you make me sound like Lucrezia Borgia!'

'You just killed my husband!'

There was silence.

'Jane, I know you're very upset,' said Honoria, 'this is upsetting for all of us, but I don't think this is an outcome anyone intended . . .'

Neil did not know why he looked at Daniel when Honoria said this, but he did, and what he saw he had seen before.

Daniel and Neil were in the study.

'What was that about?' said Neil.

'What was what about?'

'Your look of nearly imperceptible scepticism. Not imperceptible to me.'

Daniel said, 'Not "an outcome anyone intended" . . .'

'Yes, that's what made me look. To see how it went down. You think this an outcome someone intended?'

'I don't know. It could just be an unfortunate combination of things.'

'That's plausible. You know about the Swiss cheese theory, Dan?'

'No, I don't think so.'

'Accidents happen when a number of safeguards misalign in an unforeseen way. Imagine slices of Swiss cheese with holes in. Shuffle them, rearrange them in a certain way, a set of holes lines up and something can get through that otherwise wouldn't have. Maybe what's what happened with Victor?'

'His undeclared allergy, Mum's undeclared mace, a lapse of diligence by Jane?'

'And he tries the bread sauce and, without knowing, ingests an allergen that produces a fatal reaction.'

'What do the paramedics think?' Daniel asked.

'Cardiac arrest. Probably triggered by a reaction to the mace in the bread sauce – looks like he was allergic to nutmeg – with alcohol a factor, maybe physical exertion?'

'Charades is hardly a marathon.'

'He was quite strenuously handled under the mistletoe.'

Daniel said, 'Not something I'll easily forget. Did you see him actually have any bread sauce?'

'No. I don't remember. Why would I? What about you?'

'I didn't see, but I don't think he would have.'

'Because he would be wary of something he hadn't had before?' said Neil.

'Not for that reason, no.'

'You're being mysterious, Dan. Why do you think he didn't?'

'The Book of Exodus. I think it's chapter twenty-three.'

They gathered in the drawing room. It was dark outside now, the fire glowed red, the lights gleamed on the Christmas tree. Audrey had brought in tea on a trolley with the Christmas cake and a block of Wensleydale.

Jane looked sadly at the spot in front of the fire where Victor had died. It was now occupied by Cosmo and Hilda, who lay in a V-shape, their bellies turned towards the flame. Cosmo was snoring.

Jane said, 'Could we get this over with? I want to go home.'

'I'm sorry to put you through this, but I need us all here to clarify a couple of things,' said Neil.

'And there are refreshments,' said Audrey, to whom the matter of a guest's sudden demise was no reason to curtail the full ceremony of the day. So, Christmas cake with Wensleydale, an innovation Daniel had introduced to the Clement family Christmas after living in Yorkshire, was distributed, and after everyone had resolved the peculiarly English challenge of managing side plates, cake forks, cups and saucers and teaspoons while sitting on a sofa, Neil began.

'It's not confirmed yet, but it looks like Mr Cabot had an allergic reaction to the bread sauce' – Audrey was suddenly fascinated by the firelight when he said this and did not look up to see the accusing glance from her guest. 'It wasn't the first time he had reacted badly to whatever it is in nutmeg and mace, but unfortunately it caused a heart attack. It would be very helpful to know if anyone actually saw him take any bread sauce?'

No one said anything. Then Jane said, 'Yes, I did. He'd had it before, here, on a shooting weekend, only it wasn't fatally toxic.'

Audrey said nothing.

Jane went on, 'He took some today. He looked at me to see if I thought it was OK, and of course I did, so I nodded. Didn't think anything of it.'

'Are you sure?' Neil asked.

'Quite sure.'

Daniel said, 'I don't think that can be right.'

'Excuse me?'

'I suspect your husband would not have tried any bread sauce.'

Jane tutted. 'You know, Daniel, your instinct to exonerate your mother and her bread sauce is to your credit, but let us deal with the facts. He had no reason to think it was dangerous.'

'That's right.'

'So what's the damn problem?'

'It wasn't kosher.'

There was silence.

'What do you mean?' said Jane, sounding for the first time uncertain.

'Exodus, chapter twenty-three, verse nineteen: "*Thou shalt not seethe a kid in his mother's milk.*" I just looked it up.'

'And what does that have to do with anything?' she asked.

'Jewish dietary law forbids mixing meat and milk. Like venison and bread sauce. Victor was Jewish, I think?'

There was another silence. Then Jane said, 'So what? It wasn't something he went on about. It wasn't a big part of his life.'

'Until recently,' said Daniel. 'It had started to

become something he took seriously. Going to shul, observing the Law?'

'Cabot,' said Alex, 'isn't that a Boston Brahmin name? One of the first families?'

There was yet another silence.

Then Jane said, 'Kabotchnik. Russian. Victor's family arrived on a boat. During the pogroms. They arrived at Ellis Island as Kabotchniks and came out the other end as Cabots. Immigration officials too lazy to get the name right. Often happened.'

'So Victor was Jewish?' said Bernard. 'I just thought he was American. Why didn't you say anything? Mrs Shorely would have got in . . . smoked salmon . . . rather than waving her awful sausages under his nose at breakfast.'

'Thank you, Bunny, that's precisely why someone might want to keep their Jewishness quiet,' said Jane. 'Not quite right, not one of us, the wrong kind of old country.'

'I mean nothing of the sort,' Bernard blustered, but then was quiet and took a slurp of tea.

'His family settled in New York,' said Jane, 'got into real estate, made their fortune. Not their fault if people came to assume they were Gentiles.'

'But he was observant?' said Daniel.

'Yes, quietly. Would you dance round Central

Park singing "Hava Nagila" if you'd seen your people massacred in a pogrom? And then you escape to a place where Jews don't get into country clubs, and you make some money, and begin to rise. Why wouldn't you keep it quiet?'

'Yes, I can see that,' said Daniel.

'So, if Cousin Victor was so good at passing for a Gentile, Dan, how did you know he wasn't?' said Alex.

'Hymn books.'

'I don't follow.'

'At church this morning I noticed that whenever Victor went to open his hymn book, he opened it from the back, not the front.'

'I still don't follow,' said Alex.

'Hebrew is printed from right to left, so in the synagogue all the books begin at what we call the back. We had a conversation last night after Midnight Mass and Victor said he had started to rediscover his faith. I imagine he was just doing what he always did when he went to worship.'

'So he was Jewish,' said Jane, 'well spotted. And we didn't want that to be known, so thank you for embarrassing us in front of everyone.'

'Being Jewish is nothing to be embarrassed about,' said Theo.

'Thank you,' said Jane, 'I think I know that. I married one.'

Neil said, 'So he would not have eaten the bread sauce?'

'Apparently not,' said Jane.

'Then how did he come into contact with the allergen?'

'You had bread sauce, Jane,' said Daniel.

'Of course I did, after all that build-up. And it's good, Audrey,' she nodded at her. 'But it's not foie gras.'

'I could see you liked it,' said Audrey, 'you were first to help yourself, a lovely big ladle's worth. And your curiosity about the recipe was so flattering!'

Jane shrugged.

'You remember, dear? I found you busying yourself in the kitchen. When you said you were going to fetch a jug of water?'

Neil said, 'The mace?'

'It was next to the Aga,' said Audrey.

Neil said, 'Did you know there was mace in the bread sauce?'

'No. I got cloves, I got bay, but I didn't get mace,' said Jane. 'But this is ridiculous! And in very poor taste!'

'You kissed him,' said Miss March. 'Under the mistletoe.'

'A wife can't kiss her husband under the mistletoe at Christmas?'

'That's how he came into contact with the allergen. By kissing you,' said Daniel.

Jane looked around the room. 'Ridiculous. He reacted to a tiny pinch of mace in a mouthful of bread sauce eaten half an hour before he kissed me?'

'It was quite a kiss,' said Audrey, 'rather a grown-up sort of kiss . . .'

Neil interrupted. 'It can take only a tiny amount, especially when you have already had a bad reaction to it. You said Victor nearly died after drinking eggnog?'

'But that was years ago, and he didn't nearly *die* – pure hyperbole – he just . . . wheezed a bit.' Jane looked round the room. 'I didn't know there was mace in it!'

Christmas night would not be Christmas night without bathos. After the anticipation of Christmas Eve, and the festivities of the day, and the gathering of the clan with its delight and dismay, there follows washing up, tidying away, the departure of guests, and on BBC One, where once Morecambe and Wise promised diversion, Agatha Christie now awaited – not with a vintage mystery, for they had run out of those by the end of the 1980s. That was not so great a deficit in Champton Rectory, though, for they had their own to consider.

The Champton House party had left while the two kinds of tea – India or China? – were still cooling in their pots. It is not unusual for Christmas guests to accelerate to the door of departure, for few things make more demands on goodwill than the season that so relentlessly proclaims it. This departure, however, was downright urgent, for speculation that one of your guests has killed another would test the hospitality of Emerald Cunard, and Audrey all but shoved them towards the door, not that they needed encouragement.

In the kitchen, Miss March washed and Neil dried in mutually elected silence. Theo, muted, put away. Audrey went for a lie down and Daniel tidied up but had not yet got to the hall when Miss March left, so she noticed that her carefully chosen and wrapped presents for the Champton House party had been left on the bench by the front door. She was tempted to ask for them back but resisted, not wanting to leave a little coda of reproach to the doom that had ruined the day so spectacularly.

The fire in the drawing room was all but out as Theo and Audrey, now revived, settled in front of the television. Neil and Daniel retreated to the study. They were sitting opposite each other, Daniel in his armchair, Neil on the Sofa of Tears, with Cosmo and Hilda curled up on either side of him. Neil had insisted on pouring them both a Baileys from the bottle he had brought for the feast.

'Do you think she knew about the mace?' said Neil.

'Yes, don't you?'

'I do. Do you think she meant to kill him?'

'At best it's unbelievable recklessness,' said Daniel. 'At worst it's a highly ingenious murder.'

'Why would she want to kill him?'

'I don't know. There are, of course, countless married couples feeling murderous by sunset on Christmas Day, but few indulge it.'

'Money?' said Neil.

'I think that likely, although Victor was hardly parsimonious. Perhaps she has another husband in mind. Alex said she has always married up. Started with an Honourable with a mews in Mayfair, left him for a banker with a brownstone on the Upper West Side in the Swinging Sixties, left him for

Victor, who inherited a chunk of the Upper West Side, and now?'

'Is there a spare Kennedy knocking about? A Rockefeller? A Vanderbilt?'

Daniel shrugged. 'Honoria would know.'

'I'll leave you to pursue that line of inquiry, if you don't mind.'

Daniel took a sip of his Baileys. 'Oh, goodness, it's like a liquid pudding.'

'Do you like it?'

'Too early to tell. If it is murder – and that assumes rather a lot – she's got away with it, hasn't she?'

'Probably,' said Neil. 'Hard to see how any accusation would stand up. Unless, of course, she was stricken with conscience and confessed, preferably to me rather than you.'

'I don't think either of us will be troubled with that.'

They sat in silence, save a gentle snore from Hilda and the occasional knocking from the rectory plumbing, unused to the high demand placed upon it by the boiler, which Audrey had stoked extravagantly for the feast.

'Most murders go unpunished, don't you think?' said Daniel.

'I do. Most murders are undetected.'

Daniel nodded. 'A fall. A mishap by the river. A moment's forgetfulness with medication.'

'A misunderstanding with mace.'

'Yes, precisely.'

'Doesn't the blood of the murdered cry out from the earth?' said Neil.

'Sometimes. Quite a lot just seeps unnoticed into the topsoil, I think.'

'And that's that?'

'No,' said Daniel. 'In the end we are all account-able to God. But I would say that, wouldn't I?'

'And what about Jane Cabot?'

'Her too; guilty or not guilty, it will all come out in the end. But I think we may have to wait for her appearance in front of the judge of all things, rather than the Braunstonbury bench.'

Jane was finally alone at the end of that unforgettable Christmas Day. Bernard had put her in the Chinese Silk bedroom, her favourite, and with a bathroom next door assigned to the Cabots' sole use, but she had caused a fuss for Mrs Shorely because she loathed the cold and wanted the bedroom fire lit. It had been a while since a fire was last lit there, and Mrs Shorely said if it smoked it might spoil what was left of the tattered silk hangings that had been fading and fraying since the reign of George I. Jane said nothing but smiled her steeliest smile, and Mrs Shorely grudgingly laid and lit the fire, but with the caveat that there was not the staff these days to keep it lit so Jane would have to take care of it herself. It had gone out overnight, and then Mrs Shorely was called away, and now just ashes lay in the grate. We are but dust and ashes, thought Jane, and she shivered.

The room was cold. She silently cursed the land of her birth, with its terrible plumbing and endless discomforts and narrowness and tax, but that made her irritable. She decided to go down to the kitchen, if she could remember where it was, and make herself a hot milk to wash down a Valium. It would help her into her first night of widowhood.

She put on her fur and a pair of cashmere slippers and took her bag – classic Chanel, quilted beige lambskin, birthday present from Victor – and went down the great staircase. The hall was lit only by the lights on the Christmas tree, and in that empty space the light it cast looked sinister rather than comforting. She found the entrance to the service quarters and went carefully down the corridor, for suede-soled cashmere was not ideal on lino.

In the kitchen she took a pint of milk from the fridge and poured it into a milk pan so ancient the bottom had acquired a patina that looked like something from the fossil age. She put it on the hotplate and thought of nothing at all until the milk began to bubble at the edges. She poured it into a kitchen mug, left the dirty pan on the side for someone else to deal with, and sat at the plain kitchen table. She took a sip of her milk – too hot – so left it to cool and unclipped her bag to get her Valium. Two tablets, ten milligrams, she decided, under the circumstances.

There was something else in her bag next to her tablets and she took that out too and laid it on the table in front of her. She popped the tablets from the strip, put them on her tongue, took a sip of milk and down they went. She had twenty minutes or so before the effects would be felt; she wanted to be in bed before that and there was one more thing to do first.

She remembered when she was thirteen how her mother came to her room one evening to explain the change that would soon come upon her and what to do about it when it arrived. She knew anyway, because older girls at school had told her, but she sat through this unwelcome conversation without flinching. There was another unwelcome conversation when she was invited to spend the holidays at Champton, and her mother told her that among the customs of the house was the method of disposal of sanitary towels if 'one's time' should arrive while there. 'Put them in a paper bag, and after everyone's gone to bed, take them to the boiler room next to the entrance to the kitchens, open the hatch to the boiler carefully – use the special mitten that hangs on the hook there – and toss them in.'

This Jane had done, and once met another cousin doing the same thing. They disposed of their paper bags without saying a word. The ritual disposal of things defiled, she thought; it sounded quite Jewish. Perhaps Victor would have started laying down the Law and keeping a kosher household, and they would have to put in a milk kitchen and a meat kitchen. She wouldn't have minded that so much; she liked doing up kitchens. It was another cornerstone of the ancient faith that she really stumbled over. Almsgiving. When she had looked it up she had discovered that faithful Jews were expected to give generously to charity. Really generously, endowing libraries and hospitals and colleges. What a drain that would have been on resources – resources she had plans for. Religion, she thought, tutting, especially late-onset religion, messing everything up.

She looked again at the object on the table in front of her. If you did not know what it was, you would think it a marker pen, with a barrel and a tip covered by a cap, but it was not that. She picked it up and went carefully along the corridor towards the boiler room. Would it still be the same boiler? she wondered. Years had gone by since she'd needed it to dispose of a sanitary towel, but there had been no improvement in the heating since her girlhood, so she thought it reasonable to suppose the boiler was unchanged too.

There had been improvements, however, in the treatment of allergies – the most recent had given Victor new peace of mind when he became one of the first to be provided with it only a year or so ago.

There had been improvements too in boiler technology since then. Champton House's was oil-fired now, as it turned out, and there was no hatch to open, and no bed of glowing coals on which to toss one's leavings. That was disappointing. But in the boiler room there was also an ash bin, one of the old metal ones with the grooves on the sides and a scalloped lid. She lifted it and saw that it was half filled with ashes from the library fire, which, she supposed, would be going thence to the tip.

She looked at Victor's auto-injector. 'EPIPEN' it

said on the barrel. She kept one in her bag wherever they went so that, should he accidentally eat something and have an allergic reaction, she could remedy it at once by sticking the needle into his leg to release a spurt of adrenaline. What a brilliant idea – so simple, so easy to use, life-saving.

She pushed it into the ashes as deep as she decently could and replaced the bin's lid.

Then she went to the sink and washed her hands.

Audrey's Bread Sauce

1 large onion, peeled and left whole
10 whole cloves
2½ pints (1 litre) whole milk
½ teaspoon or two blades of mace
2 bay leaves
1 teaspoon of salt
8 black peppercorns
8oz (110g) freshly made white breadcrumbs from a
  good loaf
2oz (50g) butter
3 tablespoons of double cream
salt and freshly milled black pepper

1. Stud the onion with the cloves and place in a saucepan with the milk and bring to the boil with the mace, bay leaves, salt and peppercorns. Once it comes to the boil, remove from the heat and leave for at least one hour to infuse.
2. When the milk has had time to absorb the flavours, strain the milk and discard the herbs and spices, then add the soft white breadcrumbs to the milk. Place in the top half of a bain-marie, fill the bottom of the saucepan with water and gently simmer for an hour.
3. Ten minutes before you want to serve, add the butter and cream and stir. Place in a warmed jug or lidded bowl with a spoon to serve.

Acknowledgements

Juliet Annan and everyone at Weidenfeld & Nicolson
   Tim Bates and everyone at PFD
   Kitty Muirden
   Linda Grant
   Kate Albert

Discover the first novel in the
Canon Clement series . . .

From *Sunday Times* bestselling author,
The Reverend Richard Coles

www.richardcoles.com

Discover the second novel in the
Canon Clement series . . .

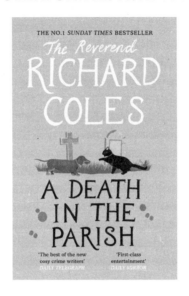

From *Sunday Times* bestselling author,
The Reverend Richard Coles

www.richardcoles.com

Discover the third novel in the
Canon Clement series . . .

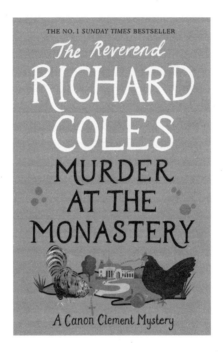

From *Sunday Times* bestselling author,
The Reverend Richard Coles

www.richardcoles.com